TOO LONG THE WINTER

◇

ROBERT PEECHER

For information the author may be contacted at

PO Box 967; Watkinsville GA; 30677

This is a work of fiction. Any similarities to actual events in whole or in part are purely accidental. None of the characters or events depicted in this novel are intended to represent actual people.

For Jean,
Who reads first.

CONTENTS

CHAPTER 1

Old Bear Le Vrette came down to the trading post for sugar, cornmeal, coffee beans, and powder. He did not come to the store to steal a girl and to take her back up into the mountains with him, but sometimes events go awry of the plans folks make.

Anymore, Old Bear didn't much care to be among people even when the winter broke. But Old Bear needed powder and he liked to get a sack of sugar to flavor his coffee. He traded beaver pelt for the goods, and the same supplies he'd acquired the last time he came down to Coggins' store cost him two pelts more this time.

"If a man is going to go on making his way in these mountains, beaver is going to have to be more plentiful and easier to trap," Old Bear complained bitterly.

Coggins had owned this trading post for these last twelve years and was accustomed to Old Bear's belly aching. As such, Coggins paid the old timer no mind. But in his last few visits, spare as they were, Bear Le Vrette had lost all of his friendly attitude. He was just miserly and grouchy. Coggins watched the old man leave the store, stow his goods on his pack mule, and begin the trek back up into the hills. There was a time when Coggins looked forward to Old Bear's occasional visits. He brought with him harrowing stories of near escapes from encounters with bear or cougar and comedic tales of trading with Indians or helping lost or stranded tenderfoots. He had always been a congenial customer welcome at the store. But these days, Coggins hoped each visit from Old Bear might be the last. The old trappers were dying off. Some were found in their cabins, but most just never came down again after a winter and folks just figured they'd died in the hills. Coggins would not be sorry when Bear Le Vrette never came down again.

Old Bear was wearing a heavy bearskin coat even though the weather was warming, and he looked for all the world like some great big, two-legged beast leading a mule up the path toward the hills. Coggins walked out to the door, and from the covered porch of the trading post he watched Old Bear mosey up the path.

There were not many people about. Seth Hanson and his son were over to the side of the store loading supplies into Hanson's wagon, and Seth's daughter was running back and forth along the path with Boots, the motley colored dog that hung around the store. The girl was not but about twelve years old, but she was tall and slender and had pretty features. Anyone who took the time to notice knew, too, that she had the prettiest blue eyes, blue like the sky on a crystal clear day. Coggins decided it would not be long before she was a pretty, young woman in this place full of both beauty and desolation.

Seth Hanson and his family were coming out of their third winter after settling in the valley. Seth did a bit of hunting and trapping, but he was a new breed of mountain man, a farmer trying to make his way on cheap land in the territory. He brought with him a family to this hostile and untamed land, and that further separated Seth Hanson and men like him from the trappers, hunters, scouts, and guides who previously wrestled for control of this land against the Injuns and the winters, the mountain cliffs and the wildlife. Coggins did not give much chance to the family men.

These ruminations were occupying Coggins' mind when he realized that Boots had gone to barking, and the Hanson girl was making a fuss. The scene unfolding before him made no sense to Coggins. Old Bear Le Vrette, ornery as he was but never cruel nor mean, had hold of the Hanson girl and was dragging her with him. She was pulling hard against Bear, but he was too strong for her.

Coggins did not think Bear Le Vrette would do him harm, and so he did not hesitate to rush to the girl's aid. They were nearly to the path leading into the woods, perhaps fifty or sixty yards from the store, and Coggins had not run so far in many years. He was winded and wiping his bald head with a handkerchief when he got to Bear.

"Come on now, Bear," Coggins said once he had his breath.

"Mr. Coggins!" Lilly Grace Hanson screamed. "Help me!"

"Bear, now, just unhand her. What do you mean by this?" Coggins reached out and took hold of Lilly Grace's other wrist and tugged against Bear's grip.

Le Vrette did not release the girl, but he turned on Coggins. There existed a rage in his voice and an anger in his eyes that Coggins did not recognize. "Turn loose a Caroline!"

3

With a quickness one would not expect from a man so old, Le Vrette unsheathed a knife from his belt and plunged it into Coggins' chest. The storekeeper stumbled backwards, looking down at the knife hilt protruding from his chest. "Damnation, Bear," Coggins said out of surprise more than anything. "You have stabbed me."

Coggins slipped from his feet and fell to his knees. He put his hands on the ground and fell over onto his back. He found it hard to breathe and he did not know what to do. "Bear Le Vrette!" Coggins called. "Come back here and help me!"

But Coggins turned his head in time to see the man, the mule, and the girl disappear into the darkness of the spruce forest. The dog was of no assistance. Coggins called to him, but the dog ran off back toward the store. Coggins wished now he had been kinder to the dog, for he would like to have some company, even if it was just the company of an old mutt. But Bear Le Vrette and the girl had gone off, and the dog had run off, and Coggins was alone.

Coggins struggled to breathe for several minutes, and hot tears were rolling from the corners of his eyes down past his temples. He looked up at the sky and wondered how he would recover with a five inch blade in his chest. After a few minutes, he heard the Hanson boy calling for his pa, and in a minute or two more, Seth Hanson knelt over him with a worried expression.

"Bear Le Vrette has stabbed me in the chest," Coggins said.

"Where's my daughter, Coggins?" Seth Hanson asked.

Coggins blinked. He had forgotten about the girl. "Bear Le Vrette took her up into the mountains. He called her

Caroline, but that ain't her name. He grabbed her and took her with him. I tried to stop him, but he stabbed me. Mr. Hanson, you've got to get me some help. Take me into the store and get me some help."

CHAPTER 2

Luther Corbett sat with his legs crossed on a stone outcrop overlooking the cabin. He did not move as he watched the men riding through the open meadow. For a bit he lost sight of them when they came under the thick canopy of the tall spruce trees intermingled with aspen, the aspen bright green with spring, the spruce their ever dark green. The little creek sprang from the ground not far above the cabin, but it filled up its banks now as the snow melt mixed with it. It took the horsemen a few moments to find the right ford that would get them safely across the creek. From his vantage, Luther could see them as they crossed the creek and again when they came into the clearing near the cabin.

Luther built his log cabin inside the big arc of a steep rock wall so that men could approach him from only the one direction. Luther liked it that way. He didn't like visitors to surprise him. Though it had been almost a year since he'd last had a visitor, and then it was just Old Bear Le Vrette. Old Bear was a Canadian who'd been up in these mountains since before Luther was born. When Luther

Corbett first came to the mountains seeking solitude and peace, Bear had treated him well, teaching him how to trap and hunt and how to survive the cold winters. As Luther pondered it, he came to realize that in the six years he'd been in among the mountains, Old Bear Le Vrette was the only visitor he'd ever had. Luther Corbett lived in a well-situated cabin.

But now there were two horsemen riding into the clearing.

The men were both armed with rifles and six shooters.

Luther made no effort to hide himself, but the men did not see him sitting on the stone ledge. He was near enough that he could hear what they said as they approached the cabin.

"Do you suppose this is it?" one of the men said.

"One way to find out," the other answered. He cupped his hands at his mouth and yelled at the cabin, "Luther Corbett! We've come to have a word. Would you come out and parley?"

Sally was in the cabin, but Luther knew she would not come out, nor would she make any answer to these men.

"Maybe he ain't here. Maybe it's the wrong cabin." This was the first man again. He struck Luther as being a bit anxious.

"If he ain't here, he'll be back soon enough, I expect," the other man said.

"We're wasting time. What if he's out on a hunt and won't be back for a week or a month? How long will we wait?"

The other man seemed perturbed. "Look here, if he shows back up he could save us valuable time. It's worth the wait of a couple of hours."

"Maybe he's in there and just ain't answering. Maybe he didn't make it through the winter and he's laying dead in his bed."

"I'll have a look," the second man said. He slid down out of his saddle, and when he did, his coat fell open and Luther noticed a metal badge of some kind pinned to his chest.

The man with the badge went to cabin door and hollered again. "Luther Corbett? I'm a federal marshal and I've rid up here to have a word with you."

The shutters on the windows were closed, but that didn't keep the marshal from trying to look in between the gap where the shutters didn't quite meet. Luther knew he wouldn't see nothing. Even with a small fire in the rock fireplace, the cabin was dark as night, except for where the cracks between some of the logs let in some beams of light. The melting snow stole some of the mud that closed those gaps. He'd have to mud up those cracks this summer to keep out the winter's cold, but that was a chore better left for late in the summer. For now, those cracks would help to let in a breeze when the summer days got hot.

The man who called himself a marshal spent some time examining the metal traps hanging on the outside wall of the cabin. He looked at the sawhorse and the piled up firewood, much diminished after a cold winter. He ran a thumb over the blade of the ax hanging on the wall. Now the marshal went back to the cabin door, and he pulled the door open to peer inside. A bearskin hanging in the doorway prevented the marshal from seeing anything. He pushed away the bearskin and leaned into the doorway.

"He'll wish he hadn't done that," Luther said to no one, and he could not help but smile.

The marshal had his head and shoulders inside the door for just a moment while his eyes adjusted, and then he hollered, "Holy Hell!" and fell backwards, slamming shut the door as he fell. Just then there was an explosion as a shotgun blast from inside the cabin splintered the door and blasted it back open. The lead balls tore holes in the bearskin hanging in the doorway.

Luther Corbett leaned forward a bit to get a better view of the marshal, who was now spread eagle on the ground in front of the door. He'd not been hit by the shotgun blast, but it had scared him good.

The anxious man on the horse drew his pistol. "What happened? Are you hit?"

"There's a damn woman with a shotgun setting in there!" the marshal said.

Luther Corbett stood up on the rock ledge where the men would be able to see him better, and he called down to them. "I would advise you not to go sticking your nose into my cabin again," he said.

"Are you Luther Corbett?" the marshal asked, shielding his eyes from the sun and looking up at the rock ledge.

"That's the name they call me by," Luther said.

"Will you come down here so we can have a talk with you?" the marshal asked.

"If I don't, will you leave?"

"Please, Mr. Corbett," the anxious man said. "We've come a long way to speak with you, and we are in a desperate hurry."

"Just hold your horses," Corbett said. "It'll take a minute to come down there. And while I make my way, I'll ask you again not to stick your head into my cabin. Sally's a bit skittish, and I know for a fact she's got another barrel loaded. You stick your head back in there, and she's liable to pull the other trigger. She's such a poor shot there ain't no telling what she might tear up next. That there was a good bearskin, and now it is ridden with holes."

The two newcomers examined the cabin. It was roughly built, and they wondered at how a man and woman could survive the cold winters in a cabin that so readily leaked air. Beside the cabin there was a small stable which looked better constructed than the house. Two horses, a couple of mules, and some goats grazed on the grass in the corral beside the stable. With the stable door open, the marshal could see there were tools hanging on the wall inside the stable and, to his surprise, what appeared to be a good buckboard wagon. The marshal looked back at the growth of aspen and spruce and wondered how Corbett ever got the wagon in and out of here. There was no path he could see that was wide enough for a wagon.

To get back down to the cabin, Luther Corbett had to walk a narrow path along the rock face and then make his way through the spruce down a steep incline and then come from around the curved stone face of the cliff. After several minutes, Luther came into the clearing.

The marshal sized him up. Corbett was tall and lean. He wore a tattered wool coat that the marshal immediately recognized as a Union cavalry officer's coat. The talk of

Luther Corbett down in the valley had him as a Confederate veteran, not a Union man. Corbett had a thick beard and long hair that fell out from below his black cavalry hat. He had bright, clear blue eyes, and the marshal guessed he was not more than thirty or thirty-five years behind his shaggy brown beard.

"Were you in the war, Corbett?" the marshal asked.

"I was," Corbett said.

"You fight for the Union?"

"I fought for my friends who kneeled down beside me behind them breastworks, marshal. That's all I fought for. Was you in the war, marshal?"

"I was not," he said. "I was working as a town marshal in Denver. And now I'm a deputy United States marshal, which means I represent the law in this territory."

"I don't mean to be disagreeable, marshal, but the law here in this territory ain't got nothing to do with the United States government. In this territory, the law is up to the river and the forest, the blizzard and the wind, the bear and the cougar and the wolves. In these mountains, the law is the rifle and the knife. The law out here is the Ute and the Shoshone. The law is the warmth you can find, or the cold that finds you."

The marshal took a cigar from his pocket, struck a match on his thumb, and lit the cigar. "Civilized men are coming to the territory, Corbett. The law is changing."

Luther Corbett took a bite of chaw, chewed on it thoughtfully for a moment, and then spit black juice into the dirt path. "Marshal, I saw in the war how civilized men is. I reckon I have seen more than I care to of what you call civilized."

The anxious man, who was still sitting his horse, slid down out of the saddle. "We didn't come here to talk about none of this," he said. "Marshal, we're losing time. Get on with it."

"Corbett, this here is Seth Hanson," the marshal said. "He's got a farm down below in the valley. Yesterday he and his son and daughter were at the Coggins trading post, getting supplies for the spring plant. Bear Le Vrette was there. I'm told you know Old Bear pretty well."

"I do know him," Luther said. "I suppose Old Bear would have to determine for hisself how well I know him."

"Well, Bear grabbed Hanson's twelve year old daughter."

"What do you mean he grabbed her?" Luther asked.

"I mean he abducted her. He kidnapped her. And when Coggins rushed out to try to stop him, Old Bear stabbed Coggins in the chest and left him to die."

Luther spit tobacco juice. "That sure don't sound like something Bear Le Vrette would do."

"Coggins identified him before he died."

"Who'd he identify him to?" Luther asked.

"Me," Seth Hanson said. "I was around to the side of the trading post loading supplies in my wagon. I was nearly done, so I sent my son to fetch my daughter. He come back and said she was gone and that Coggins was lying in the road with a knife in him. I went out to Coggins, and he told me he seen Bear Le Vrette take my daughter, and when he tried to stop him, that's when Le Vrette put that knife in his chest. Coggins said Le Vrette told him to keep his hands off 'Caroline,' but my daughter's name is Lilly

Grace."

"And Coggins is dead?" Luther asked.

"He is," the marshal said.

Luther Corbett would not have believed these strangers, except that Hanson mentioned the name 'Caroline.' It was a name Bear Le Vrette had said to Luther when the men were on long hunts together.

"I'm sorry for your troubles," Corbett said to Hanson. "But I reckon I don't see what any of this has to do with me."

"We've come to ask your help," the marshal said. "We need to find Le Vrette and get the girl back. Folks say you're the only one around here who knows these mountains as well as Le Vrette."

Luther Corbett looked over the marshal's shoulder at the tall cypress trees and the Quaking Aspen, all golden-green with spring growth.

"I ain't a tracker," Corbett said. "And I sure don't know the mountains as well as Old Bear."

"But you know where he lives? You know how to find his cabin?" Seth Hanson took a step forward. Luther could tell the man was desperate over his daughter.

"I know how to find his cabin," Luther confirmed.

"Then we need you to take us there. And as fast as possible. We need to try to get to my daughter before any harm comes to her."

Luther spit the chaw from his mouth. "Sally don't like it none when I chew," he explained. "Y'all wait here while I speak to her."

Luther Corbett bought Sally from a Ute chief two years before. He never was sure about her heritage but thought she was part squaw and part Mexican. Whatever she was, she'd been a slave among the Ute for some time. She could not say how long, and Luther could not guess. He traded an old musket for her. She was skittish when she first come to live with him because the Indians had used her poorly, but when she came to understand that Luther wasn't going to beat her, she warmed up a bit. She still didn't talk much, and Luther wasn't sure if the Indians hadn't broke something in her mind, but she could be compelled to laugh sometimes and she didn't object when Luther laid atop her, and she was warm when the snow piled up and the cold wind whipped through the trees. Luther thought of her as a wife, but he did not know if she thought of him as a husband. When he went off for days and weeks at a time to trap and hunt, she was always there at the cabin waiting when he got home. So he figured she didn't mind him too much. He did not know her given name, but he liked the name Sally and called her that, and she never did disagree with him about it.

"Sally, girl, these men you shot at need me to take them up to Old Bear Le Vrette's cabin. I'll be gone two or three days."

Sally didn't say anything. She'd put down the shotgun when she heard Luther talking to the men outside. She was now putting a log onto the fire in the fireplace. The weather outside was pleasant, neither cold nor hot. Luther himself would not have had a fire going on this day, but Sally liked to have a fire most all of the time.

"If you have a mind to it, you might see if you can sew up them holes you shot into the bearskin. That's a good skin, and it fits the door well."

Sally watched him talk but did not speak back, either to agree or argue a point. Even with the fire going, it was dark in the cabin. It smelled musty, too, having been closed up all through the winter.

"You might want to open up the shutters, too, for a little while, and let it air out in here. Maybe hang some of them blankets on a line outside and let them air out, too."

The floor of the cabin was just dirt with bearskins put down on it. "The bear rugs might stand some time on the line as well."

She still did not speak, but Luther stepped over to her and kissed her on the forehead. It was a custom he'd learned from his own mother when he was a boy, and he sometimes felt compelled to kiss Sally on the forehead in the same way. She never did seem to appreciate it, but she did not attempt to avoid it, either. "I hope you'll be here when I get back, but if you decide you want to leave, I'll understand that. And if you do leave, I'll miss your company when you're gone."

Sally reached up a hand and pressed it against Luther's bearded cheek. "Tell Bear I said hello," she said.

Luther smiled at her, but his expression was sad. "I'll do it."

Poor Sally was like a beat dog. Too skittish and unsure to even accept a kindness, but too helpless to go off on her own. Luther Corbett did not like to think how them Injuns must have treated her to make her so. Luther figured one day he'd go off on a hunt and return to find she'd gone down to be among the people. And that was all right with him. He'd gotten use from her equal to that of a smooth bore musket.

Luther saddled the painted horse that was in the corral. The paint was the better of the horses for mountain riding. It had surer feet, and Luther never knew it to slide or stumble on a rocky incline. He led the way out of the clearing and through the stand of spruce and aspen, through the ford of the swollen creek, and out into the grass of the meadow. There, in the big meadow, he urged the paint horse forward at a quicker pace. Most of the way to Old Bear Le Vrette's cabin would be slow going, back and forth over switchbacks, up and down steep inclines where they would have to lead the horses, and over rocky terrain where the horses would have to go slow for fear of losing footing on the loose rocks. They would go beyond the tree line and through a pass, and then down into the valley where Old Bear Le Vrette made his home away from people. Old Bear did not ride a horse and so he did not live in a place where horses could easily get. He led his old mule around only to have a way to carry heavy loads.

CHAPTER 3

After a long ride through the lush meadow that took the three riders in a wide curve to the west, Luther came to the place he'd been aiming for. To their right was a large stand of aspen, and Luther was looking for the aspen with the curve in its trunk. When he found it, he rode in among the trees, following a barely visible deer trail. The stand of trees opened up to reveal a shallow, clear water creek that they passed through. The marshal and Seth Hanson did not realize it was the same creek that began in the spring near Luther's cabin. The creek meandered its own way through the trees, touching the meadow and then curving back in among the trees again, flowing out over rocks and down through deep ravines.

On the opposite side of the creek the vegetation turned to tall spruce, and the mountain side rose steep from there.

"We'd best walk the horses here," Luther said.

There was no trail that either the marshal or Seth Hanson could distinguish, but Luther never broke stride or seemed confused of his whereabouts. He led his horse up a long, steep incline in switchback fashion, and the marshal and Hanson followed him. Both the marshal and Hanson had lost all sense of direction. After a couple of hours of walking among the spruce in this fashion, they came out above the tree line to a high mountain meadow that was level, or level enough.

"We should camp here for the night," Luther told them. "Sun will be down in the west below the far mountains soon, and we'll quickly lose all light." Already the sun was beyond the peak that rose above them, but the sky was light enough that they could still see. Hanson was out of breath after the long walk, but he objected to camping.

"We will lose too much time if we stop now," he said. "We must press onward."

The marshal looked up at the sky. He'd already noticed it growing darker and had wondered himself about camping. The marshal and Hanson had already come a long way just to find Corbett. "Might be best if we stopped."

Luther Corbett understood Hanson's eagerness. The man believed he would have to make haste to preserve his daughter.

"This is the best ground we'll encounter for a camp," Luther said. "Flat enough and with a little grazing for the horses. If we go much farther we will be above the trees, and up higher, the wind at night would whip us to death if it didn't freeze us first. In the morning will ride up above the tree line and go through the pass. We'll come across a ridge and drop down into the forest a ways, and we will follow a youthful river down to a gulch, and that's where we'll find Bear Le Vrette's cabin."

Being outnumbered in the vote, Hanson set aside

his complaints. Luther Corbett set to work preparing a lean-to shelter to provide protection from the wind and rain should any storm kick up over night, as they often did. He used his hatchet to fell some big spruce boughs and layered these one over the other against the lean-to so that it would serve as a windbreak and also keep dry. Luther collected dry wood and made a fire near the entrance to the lean-to. Hanson took the horses to a nearby pool of snow melt and watered them. The marshal watched Corbett with interest.

"You been in these mountains long?"

"Since the end of the war," Corbett said.

"You come from back east?"

"I did. Born in the hills of Alabama."

"So you fought for the Confederacy? Where'd you get that Union coat?"

"I told you who I fought for," Luther said. He had no harshness in his tone. "The coat was gived to me by a man who no longer had need of it."

By the time the sun disappeared, the lean-to was built to Luther's satisfaction and big enough to shelter all three men. The fire crackled and popped its warmth. The men put blankets on their horses and also wrapped themselves in blankets, and then they gathered under the shelter with their faces directed toward the fire.

"You ever known Bear Le Vrette to handle women rough?" the marshal asked Corbett.

"In the time I've known him, I never did know him to handle women at all," Luther said. "He had a wife once, but that was before I come into the mountains."

19

"What do you reckon he wanted with my daughter?" Hanson asked.

Luther Corbett noted that Seth Hanson seemed to always have a hostile tone when he spoke. At first Corbett dismissed it as Hanson's urgent desire to get to his daughter, but he was beginning to wonder if Hanson did not view Corbett as complicit, somehow, in the abduction of his daughter. As a friend of Old Bear's, Hanson seemed to hold Luther accountable.

"I couldn't say," Corbett told him. "I ain't never seen Old Bear act that away. It's hard for me to believe that he put a knife in Coggins, a man we both know and trust. And I suppose it's harder for me to believe that he left the knife. Old Bear ain't the kind of man who would leave a good knife behind."

Hanson, who'd been leaning on an elbow over near the fire, sat straight up like he'd been stung. "Is that supposed to be a joke? Do you think it's some kind of joke that Bear Le Vrette killed a man and kidnapped my daughter?"

Luther was impassive. "No, sir. It ain't supposed to be a joke. I mean what I say. Bear Le Vrette ain't the sort of man would leave a good knife behind."

Hanson eyed Corbett in the light of the fire. "I aim to get my daughter back."

"We're all aiming at the same target, Mr. Hanson," Luther said. "But Old Bear is a friend of mine, and I'm puzzled why he would have done the things you said he done. It's not in his character to do such. I suppose to you it may not be important why he done it, and I can understand that. But up in these mountains, a man ain't got many friends. And when you have one, and he does something you can't make hide nor hair of, you'd like to know why."

Hanson picked up another stick and tossed it onto the fire.

"The reason why don't matter to me," Hanson said. "But when I've got my daughter, I intend to make Old Bear Le Vrette sorry he ever took her."

The marshal said, "Now, listen Seth, we ain't up here as vigilantes. I'm the law, and I intend to bring Bear back down to face trial."

"Damn the law," Hanson spat.

The marshal didn't respond.

Luther laid his head down on the Indian blanket he was using for a bed and wrapped the other half over himself. It was going to be a cold night, but Luther had spent many a cold night in the mountains.

***

As soon as there was light to travel, the three men were moving again. They followed Luther Corbett up through what remained of the thinning spruce forest, and when they were able they mounted their horses and rode out across the bare top of the mountain and through the pass. Here, above the tree line, the bald, exposed face of the mountain was still covered in snow so that the horses had to high step through it, and the gusts of wind picked up loose snow and blew it like soft clouds out over the valley. All of the men pulled scarves up over their faces and ears to protect them from the gusty wind that blew so cold. They passed by two large mountain lakes that slowly poured out into a river that cut its way down to the valley below. The men dropped back down into the forest, and here again the angle of the slope made it necessary to walk the horses rather than ride. All through the forest they could hear, even when they could not see, a gushing creek, swollen with the melting snow, as it slowly wore away at its rocky bed, fell down through open air and cascaded again over stone and between rocks. At length, they came out of the forest into a lush meadow of grass and mountain wildflowers.

Large boulders burst up out of the green meadow in spots. The sun was now directly overhead, and Luther turned his face up to it, giving him the first real warmth he'd had all day.

He mounted up on the paint horse, and the marshal and Hanson also stepped into their saddles.

"If you look down there opposite the meadow you can see a lake. On the other side of that lake is a stand of aspen, and beyond those aspen is Bear Le Vrette's cabin," Luther told them. "We will be there shortly. But I can tell you, Bear Le Vrette has a view from his cabin that allows him to see this meadow. He will know we are coming."

The marshal slid his carbine rifle, a shortened Trapdoor Springfield, from its scabbard and loaded a cartridge into the breech. He then put firing caps on each cylinder of his revolver. Hanson repeated the same process.

"There'll be no need for those firearms," Luther Corbett said. "I will speak to Bear Le Vrette and get all this straightened out."

"What makes you think he'll listen to you?" Hanson asked.

"I know Bear Le Vrette. He'll speak to me."

"You also said you've never known him to stab a man or steal a girl."

The men rode across the flat meadow and circled the mountain lake. In among the aspen they were free to ride, so they did not dismount until they came to a clearing, across which sat Le Vrette's cabin. If the marshal and Hanson were unimpressed by Luther's cabin, they were less impressed by Old Bear's home. It was partially dug into the ground so that the roof was not much taller than an average man. It had no windows, only a single entryway that would require a man to stoop down to get through. And there was no door, just a bear skin hanging over the opening.

But just like at Luther's place, there was a solidly built stable big enough for a half dozen horses. Bear at one time kept a horse or two, but now all he kept were three pack mules.

"You men like your stables, don't you?" Hanson said, looking at the place.

Luther Corbett took a bite of tobacco and spit some of the juice out.

"A man may find the only thing that can save his life up in these mountains is his horse, or in Bear's case his mule. A wise man takes good care of those things that he needs to survive."

"How do you want to do this, marshal?" Hanson said. "I can work my way around and get to the cabin from the right flank, there."

Luther Corbett heard the military talk and looked at Hanson. He'd not struck him as a man who had been in the war. Seth Hanson was a family man. But Luther conceded in his own mind that he might have guessed wrong about Hanson and that men with families now might have been men who fought before.

"There'll be no need for any of that," Luther said. "Y'all just follow me up to the cabin. I'll speak with Bear."

Luther did not mention it yet, but he believed Bear Le Vrette was not at home, and Luther believed Bear Le Vrette had no intention of returning. Bear's traps were all missing from the front of the cabin where they usually hung. Bear never took all of his mules with him, yet all three were gone. And there was no smell of smoke in the air. If Bear had been home in the morning, he'd have made a fire and cooked some breakfast. The fire might have died out by now, but the smell of smoke would have lingered.

The men rode across the clearing, and as they reined in, Luther called out.

"Bear Le Vrette! It is your friend Luther Corbett come to pay you a call! I have with me a man who says he is the law in these mountains, and a man who says you've got a girl who belongs to him. Would you come out and parley with us a bit?"

Luther noted that the marshal had his rifle setting across his lap.

"Old Bear! Come and have a word," Luther called out again.

When nothing inside the cabin stirred, Luther turned to the marshal. "I believe Old Bear has absconded."

"What makes you sure?" the marshal asked.

"Traps is all gone. Mules is all gone. I'll have a look in the cabin, but I believe I will find that it has been emptied of the important things."

Luther slid down out of his saddle and went into Bear's cabin. He held a hand out over the fireplace and looked around for good blankets, powder and ball, cooking things, flour or meal. He found none of these things. The essentials that would keep a man alive in the cold and unforgiving mountains were all missing.

"He has not been here since before supper yesterday," Luther announced when he emerged from the cabin.

"Where has he gone?" Hanson demanded.

"I could not say."

But Luther began to look around all the same. He looked in at the stable and walked around through the clearing. He followed some tracks he found out toward the stand of aspen, and there he found a branch lying on the ground. The branch was broken in two. Luther knelt down and felt the wood. The branch was dry. If it had been on the ground for any length of time, it would be wet. Luther guessed it had fallen there within the last few days, and he further guessed the weight necessary to break it would be equal to that of a mule that had trod upon it. Luther walked deeper into the aspens, and in the shady parts where the sun did not reach, he found a patch of snow still on the ground. In that snow he saw the tracks of two people, one of whom was diminutive, and at least two but probably three mules.

Luther looked back at Hanson and the marshal, and the two men seemed to be in some disagreement.

Following the tracks just a bit farther and finding confirmation of his theory, Luther Corbett reached his conclusion.

"Old Bear has gone down toward the valley," he said to Hanson and the marshal. "That is a several mile journey. I do not believe he will continue all the way into the valley where he might likely encounter people. But that is the direction he started in."

Luther stretched his face up toward the sun again, feeling its warmth. "I reckon there ain't much more I can do to help you men. I wish you luck, and I hope you find your daughter, Mr. Hanson."

"You can't leave us," the marshal said.

"You asked me to bring you to Bear Le Vrette's cabin, and I have done that," Luther said. "Now I'm going to go on back home. I've got trapping and hunting to do."

"We should go on," Hanson said. "If Le Vrette was here yesterday, he hasn't got but a day's jump on us. If we hurry, we might still catch him."

The marshal took a draw on his cigar and blew the smoke into the wind. "No, sir. You and I would not be able to track him. You're a farmer and I am a town peace officer. We are outside of our elements here in these mountains, Mr. Hanson." Now the marshal turned toward Corbett. "Luther, you've done what we asked you to do, and I'm grateful to you for it. But I'm going to have to ask you for more, I'm afraid. We need your help in tracking Old Bear. We need somebody who understands the mountains and understands the way Old Bear thinks. I could go back into town and find a Ute Injun to help us, I suppose, but we would lose two or three days. You must understand that this situation is urgent. A girl's life could be at stake."

This turn of events came as no surprise to Luther Corbett. He had anticipated the marshal would make an appeal for further assistance, but his mind was not yet made up. The winters in the mountains were long and harsh, and if he was going to have beaver and bear pelts to trade for supplies at the end of summer, he would need to get into the woods with his traps. But he knew, too, that Bear Le Vrette should not have taken the man's daughter nor stabbed Coggins, and he felt an strange sense of responsibility. And adding weight to the marshal's plea was the truth that neither the marshal nor Hanson would have any hope of finding Old Bear if he didn't want to be found.

"I'll give you two more days," Corbett said.

CHAPTER 4

The aspen woods sheltered enough snow that tracking Bear down toward the valley was not difficult. The men stayed mounted as the narrow trunks and high branches of the aspen afforded them open room for riding. But the lower down the mountain they went, the less accumulation of snow there was. At times Luther Corbett had to dismount and walk around for a bit to find some evidence — a fresh broken branch, a bit of mule leavings, a footprint in the soft, muddy ground. At length, though, the aspen forest opened into a wide meadow already overgrown with fresh grass and wildflower, and here the sun had sent away all the snow and tracks were impossible to find in the shin-high growth.

Luther Corbett stepped down out of his saddle and made a long, slow walk in the meadow looking for any sign of which way Bear Le Vrette might have gone. Several times he looked at the high ridges surrounding him, hoping for inspiration.

"He's got no idea where to go," Hanson said to the

marshal. The two men sat their horses at the edge of the aspen growth, watching Luther as he looked about.

The marshal took a draw on his cigar. "No, I reckon you're right." There was bitter disappointment in the marshal's voice. "We've lost them in the meadow here. No tracks to follow."

Luther had stopped searching the meadow and was now just looking up at the peak above him, trying to reason through what Old Bear might have done upon reaching this place. If Bear Le Vrette had taken the girl and the mules and left at noontime the previous day and gone up from the meadow, they would have spent the night up high in the bitter cold winds. If he went down toward the valley, he might encounter people, a thing he would not want to do. But his ability to camp and travel with three mules and a child was better going down than going up. If Bear understood that men would be chasing him, and surely he did, he would certainly have gone down into the valley where he could move more rapidly. After all, Luther thought, a wounded deer would go down toward the valley in search of a flowing stream.

But these contemplations were the thoughts of a man fleeing other men in haste, a desperate man with no intention of destination. These were the thoughts of a wounded deer seeking succor from the water.

Luther Corbett did not know Old Bear Le Vrette to ever be a desperate man, whether threatened by grizz or Injun or bobcat or blizzard. Pursued though he was, Bear Le Vrette was no wounded deer.

A goat would go high where it could move better than its adversary. Old Bear was like a goat.

"I suspect Bear went up from here," Luther

announced. "I am not sure of it, for I can find no trace of him in the meadow. But I think we should look for him up above."

Hanson cussed viciously. "We cannot go forward based solely upon this man's guess. He is a friend of the fugitive and might purposefully lead us astray."

The marshal looked up at the high peak above. He did not care to be caught there at night or if a storm blew in. Crossing the meadow and following the forest down into the valley would give them a better opportunity to find or make shelter at nightfall. There would be ample water going farther down, and forage for the horses. These were good reasons for going lower. But, of course, they were not seeking shelter nor water nor forage. They were seeking a man of these mountains who had committed murder and taken a child.

"Mr. Hanson, if you choose to go a different way, you are welcome to it. I'm following Corbett up to the peak."

Luther mounted his horse and circled around the outside of the meadow looking for the way up. When he found it, it wasn't more than a goat path leading back into a spruce forest, but the path was not too steep and clear enough that the men were able to stay mounted for some time. Luther continued to look for sign that would indicate he had chosen correctly, but he saw nothing. After some time they were forced to abandon the path as it went too steep and they began a series of long, slow switchbacks with no trail to follow. Luther Corbett went solely on instinct and following the grain of the land.

They had risen very high now and the trees were beginning to thin some, and yet there had been no sign of

Bear Le Vrette, the mules or the girl. Luther conceded in his mind that he might have picked wrong. He did not want to go above the tree line and cross to the east side of the mountain without having confidence in his decision. For the last hundred yards or more, he had come up with a dozen good reasons why Bear might have gone down into the valley.

But as they came to the foot of a steep, rocky cliff, something in the brush caught Luther's attention. He tied off his horse to a branch and walked down a few feet to the brush and pulled out a wide spruce branch that was sitting in among the undergrowth. The evergreen needles were still green and fresh. Luther examined the end of the branch, and it looked to him it had been shaved from a tree with a hatchet. There was fresh sap at the end where the branch had been shaved from its tree, and the sap was not filthy with dirt.

It did not take Luther but a moment to find the spruce tree from which the branch had been shaved. The exposed, white meat of the tree shone like a beacon. Luther looked at the bark and could see the evidence of the hatchet or knife cut. Now he looked for the reason that a man might cut off a branch like this.

Along the side of the stone cliff there was a slide of rocks, some the size of a fist and others the size of a goat's head. But the slide of rocks showed a way up to a good sized ledge. Growing out from the ledge were a couple of short, bushy spruce trees. It always puzzled Luther Corbett that trees would find a way to grow out of rock like that.

"I'll be a minute," Luther said to the marshal and Hanson, who had been watching him with interest but did not interrupt.

He had to scale up to the ledge using his hands and being careful where he placed his feet. In the sandy dirt he saw what appeared to be the place where a person had put their foot and had it slide on them. When he reached the ledge, Luther found that the rock was naturally hollowed out a bit. Two people might easily fit inside the hollow and be protected from the wind. But Luther no longer needed conjecture to guess at where Old Bear Le Vrette and the Hanson girl had spent the night. At the mouth of the hollow, there behind the short spruce trees, was a fire pit. Luther put his hand to it and felt just a bit of warmth. He pushed away the top layer of coals and found some at the bottom that were warm to the touch.

Now Luther scrambled back down the rock slide. Once he was back to the bottom of the rock face, Luther examined the dirty ground around them. He found what he expected to find, brush strokes. Old Bear had spent the night with the girl up on the ledge in the hollowed out rock. The mules had stayed down below. This morning, before they left out, Old Bear had cut a branch from a spruce tree and used it to brush away the tracks the mules had made overnight.

"They camped here," Luther proclaimed. If there was a tone of victory to his voice, neither the marshal nor Seth Hanson heard it. Luther just said it matter of fact, without pride.

"Both of them?" Hanson asked.

"I believe there were two," Luther confirmed.

"So he's not killed her. He still has her. We must hurry and overtake them."

The men pressed on, leading their horses toward the edge of the trees. A rumble in the distance caught

Luther's attention. They would be leaving the trees soon and emerging out onto the bald, exposed top of the mountain. The wind blew hard here, not in gusts, but constant. A have cloud or storm, with the blowing snow, could make it impossible to see on the mountain top. A misplaced foot fall could prove fatal. They might get lost with no trail to follow and walk right over the edge of a cliff. It would be bad enough in the blowing snow, but if a storm was coming in it might be impossible to press forward.

"We should wait out the storm," Luther Corbett suggested.

"We cannot wait," Hanson said. "Every moment that goes by puts my daughter in greater jeopardy. If we hope to overtake them, we cannot stop."

Luther Corbett agreed that if they waited out the storm it would give Bear Le Vrette an excellent opportunity to widen the distance between pursued and pursuers. Old Bear would be going downhill now, and while it was not easy traveling, it was likely a good deal faster.

"It does not matter how far ahead they get if we are blind up here and walk off the face of the mountain and are crushed on the rocks below," Luther said. "You men may go forward if you choose, but I will wait for the storm to pass."

The marshal quickly made up a fire while Luther Corbett skinned several spruce branches from some nearby trees to build a crude lean-to that would allow the men to shelter from the worst of the rain. He widened it out enough that the horses could find some small amount of shelter as well, at least for their heads. While they made these preparations, the thunder continued to rumble, and the cloud cover moved. Slowly, but growing in intensity, the rain began to hit the spruce branches of the shelter. Even in the summertime with the sun bathing the top of the mountain, it could be bitter cold in the wind up in the high altitude and a man might suffer from exposure. But now, in the early spring, exposure was an even more pressing threat. Luther wondered how he would proceed if one or both of these men who were unaccustomed to the higher reaches fell sick, or if he would even proceed at all.

Bear Le Vrette knew these woods and these mountains. Luther might be able to find his way, but Bear knew where he was going and how to get there. Luther Corbett did not know why his friend had grabbed Seth Hanson's daughter, but with the rain coming heavy now and the wind finding its way between the trees and the marshal and Seth Hanson both shivering, Luther Corbett began to doubt that anyone here would again see Lilly Grace Hanson.

CHAPTER 5

Lilly Grace Hanson sat deep in the lean-to shelter the old man had made of spruce branches. She was huddled in a bearskin blanket but still shivering. The rain made the cold worse. The musty smell of the bearskin added to her discomfort. It had been such a pretty day when she went with her father and brother to Coggins' store, and she wore only a light, knitted coat over her cotton dress. She was not dressed to be moving about in the high reaches of the mountains, and unaccustomed to the rocky, steep terrain. They had spent the night before in a shallow cave on a rocky ledge. The rock was uncomfortable and the wind and cold easily found her. The old man, pressed up against her, stank so bad that she had to press her nose into the bearskin. The palms of her hands and both knees were skinned from where she had fallen on rocks and scraped herself.

Her physical discomfort was mild, though, compared to the sorrow in her heart.

Lilly Grace did not understand why this man abducted her. She watched when he stabbed his knife into

Mr. Coggins, and she was terribly frightened.

When she cried, the mountain man was callous.

When she hurt herself or complained of the cold, he was indifferent.

When she prayed, he was cruel.

The first night after he took her they camped under a lean-to. The man forced her to lie down in the back of the lean-to, and he slept pressed up against her with an arm draped across her body. The second night they slept on the dirt floor of his cabin. He had no bed. Again, he slept against her and snored in her ear. The next night they slept on the rock ledge.

But with the man stretching his arm over her, and the fear and discomfort she felt, Lilly Grace slept only in fits and starts. The food he gave her was bland, and she was so scared that her stomach hurt, so she could not eat anyway.

She was out of tears, but she had not lost hope. She continued to pray and believed that salvation would come.

"Don't get too comfortable," the old man said. "We ain't staying the night here. Soon as the storm passes, we'll keep to moving."

"Where are you taking me?" Lilly Grace asked.

"We're going back to the old cabin," the man said. "We'll fix it back up and it'll be just like before."

The man said things like this, and called her by the name Caroline. Lilly Grace did not understand, but she also did not question him. The old man had not struck her, but Lilly Grace was afraid he might.

"You could take me back," she offered. "Nobody will

be mad at you if you take me back."

"We're going back to the old cabin, Caroline. I'll not hear no more of it."

"Please, mister," Lilly Grace said. "I am cold and I just want to go home."

The old man's eyes flashed angry at her, and Lilly Grace shrank back away from him.

"We are going home," the man said.

Lilly Grace felt faint. Ever since they'd been in the wind, her head was spinning. She was so tired and so hungry, and the cold bit her on the inside.

Bear Le Vrette broke a couple of green branches and pushed them into the fire. The branches would not burn well and would smoke too much, but they were too high to find good wood for a fire, so Old Bear figured he would burn what he could find.

He had not seen any sign of pursuit, but he knew men were coming behind him.

Old Bear struggled to work out what was happening. The people down below in the towns always confused him, but his confusion seemed more complete than anything he could recall. He knew men were chasing him and Caroline, but he could not recollect what sin he had committed. Pursuit was more a feeling to him now than an understanding. He felt he was being pursued, but did not understand the cause.

He worried over Caroline. She never did do well traveling in the mountains, which is why she always stayed so close to the cabin. But she seemed so frail now. Old Bear remembered a time when Caroline was more frail, when she was older, just before he lost her. He just needed to get her home to the old cabin now and she would be fine. But with her feeling so poorly, they could only move so fast. And with unseen men coming after them, it heightened Bear's agitation.

Old Bear leaned over and blew hard on the flames to get them to jump up and catch the green branches.

"Why would you stab Mr. Coggins?" Lilly Grace asked him.

Bear did not look back at her. He blew hard again on the flames.

"Huh?" he said. "Stab Coggins? I would do no such thing."

"But you did," Lilly Grace said. "You stabbed Mr. Coggins."

Bear LeVrette looked at the girl. "Don't talk nonsense," he said. "I will get this fire flamed up so that you can get some warmth, Caroline, and when the rain is gone we will keep on going."

"Why do you call me that?" Lilly Grace asked. "My name is Lilly Grace."

Old Bear picked up a branch he had sitting on the ground next to the fire and violently hit the ground with it. He rounded on her with anger burning in his eyes. "Woman, I'll have no more nonsense. You are out of your mind with a fever."

Against the violent outburst, Lilly Grace huddled deeper into the bearskin blanket wrapped around her. She whispered a silent prayer of deliverance, praying that God would send her father to come and save her. She felt ill and wanted to be home with her family.

CHAPTER 6

By the time the storm passed and the sky cleared enough that Luther Corbett felt they could safely go over the tundra, there was not much daylight that would be left. Luther knew that Hanson would be opposed to spending the night here in this camp, and the truth was that Luther also was opposed to it. He was eager to reach Bear Le Vrette and attempt to get some answer as to Bear's odd behavior. He worried over his friend, and he also did not want Old Bear to be responsible for some foul misfortune that might befall the girl.

"Marshal, kick down that fire. If we're to go on before dark, we must move now," Luther said.

As soon as the riders were beyond the tree line, they mounted their horses and rode out over the snowcap. Luther knew his paint horse and what it could endure riding in the high altitude, and he did not push it. He watched the other horses, as well, to be sure they could handle the cold and the lack of air. If one of the men had to go afoot, it would slow them all down. If they hoped to catch up to Bear

Le Vrette, they would need to use the horses as much as possible. It was likely, though, that the girl was slowing him.

The high mountain ridge seemed endless. Up in the high altitudes, distance was often a confusing thing. There was no tree as a landmark and with everything covered in snow, even the rock outcroppings did not serve. The great white sheet just seemed to stretch on forever, and a hundred yards could look like a mile or the other way round.

The terrain seemed to force the movement, though there was no clear trail. But the slope pushed the riders in what Luther hoped would be the same way that it pushed Bear Le Vrette. The wind still blew heavy and kicked up snow from the cap, and the blowing snow added to the difficulty in seeing any distance.

Luther watched for signs that Le Vrette had passed over the ridge here, but everything was white, and the rain and the blowing snow covered any tracks that might have existed.

Seth Hanson's breathing was hard when he spoke. "Do you see any sign that they came this way?"

"I do not," Luther admitted. "But Bear Le Vrette is traveling with three mules loaded with supplies and a girl who is not accustomed to traveling through these mountains. He cannot go in places that we cannot go. The man by hisself might go farther down the slope or might attempt to climb higher over the ridge, but not with those mules and not with that girl. We know that he came out on this ridge, and so we will follow the path the ridge forces a man and three mules to take."

Luther instinctively felt the moment that the ridge took them from one side of the mountain to the next and they began to drop, just a bit, lower down the other side. At length, the snow began to break and it was only in patches across the rock and tundra surface, and as the ridge continued to drop, they arrived at a spot covered in grass and wildflower. Luther Corbett slid down off of his horse and here began to look for sign. Two slopes dropped down off the ridge, and Luther believed Bear Le Vrette must surely have taken one of these slopes rather than continue out across the ridge.

"I suspect that Bear was here when he began to hear thunder rumbling," Luther said. "He might have continued along the ridge line, but I doubt it. He'd have sought shelter."

The marshal was still mounted, as was Seth Hanson. The marshal was looking down the slopes when something caught his eye. "Is that not smoke?"

Luther Corbett turned and looked. It was faint enough, but indeed he could see a small trail of smoke coming up through the trees.

Now both the marshal and Hanson were off their horses and sliding rifles from their scabbards.

"Stay here with the horses," Hanson said to Corbett. He did not wait for a reply. Both the marshal and Hanson were now scurrying down the slope toward the smoke.

Luther took the horses by their leads and started to lead them down the slope. He watched as the marshal and Hanson entered in among the spruce trees. It was too dark already for him to see deep into the woods.

Just as Luther was reaching the trees, the marshal came walking back up toward him.

"Gone," he said. "He left the fire burning, or it

kicked back up with the wind blowing. He's built a lean-to. You should look to see if you can guess how long it has been since he was here."

They tied off the horses on branches, and Luther looked around at the lean-to.

"They probably left two hours ago," he said.

"What do you see that makes you think so?" Hanson said.

"They are not here," Luther replied. "They weathered the storm here, the same as we did. The storm passed here about two hours ago. So I think they must have left about two hours ago. But they have left tracks."

Luther pointed to the muddy ground. "The mules, Bear, the girl. All clear tracks. Leaving here in a hurry was more important to him than covering his tracks. Or maybe he thinks no one is now following him. If so, that will make it easier to follow him."

"If we hurry we can catch them," Seth Hanson said.

"It will be dark soon," Luther said, and he was going to suggest that they should camp the night at Bear's lean-to. But Seth Hanson's temper exploded.

"I've had enough of this," Hanson shouted. "If not for your constant concerns about the weather or the dark, we would have caught this man by now. But at every turn, when we have nearly secured my daughter's safety, you have delayed us and stalled our pursuit so that your friend had time to go farther."

Hanson walked a circle and spat at the ground. He took his plea to the marshal, "We must continue. If Bear Le Vrette is in fact only two hours in front of us, we must continue until we have overtaken him."

"Luther has gotten us this far, which is much farther than we would have gone without him," the marshal said. "It's damned unfair to accuse him of stalling us when we have closed the gap on Bear and Lilly Grace."

Hanson pushed his face into his hands and moaned loudly. He was going mad with despair and worry over his stolen daughter.

"How much longer can you follow these tracks before we are forced to stop?" the marshal asked Luther.

Corbett looked at the rapidly dimming sky.

"Maybe we could go on another half hour. Maybe three-quarters of an hour. But if we are to get through the night, we will need shelter, and we will need light to build that shelter. Those tracks will still exist come morning, and we can follow them more quickly and farther in the light."

The marshal was a hard man. He'd shot men and men had shot at him. He was not married, nor did he have children. He enjoyed the rough life of miners and ranchers, gamblers and gunslingers. He did not know what attracted him to this life in the territory, but he liked it. And to live on the frontier, where life was violent, a man had to limit how much he concerned himself with other people's affairs. As a marshal, folks came to him with their troubles frequently. He helped where he was duty bound, but he avoided feeling too much over the sorrows that plagued other people.

"Listen here, Mr. Hanson," the marshal said. "Luther Corbett knows these mountains in a way that you and I do not. Now, I'm out here helping you to get your daughter back. But if we press on when Luther says we should not and we get lost or lose the trail or walk up on a grizzly in the middle of the night, ain't none of that going to help your daughter. If Luther says we stop, then I stop. If you want to press on and give chase in the dark, you'll have to do it on your own."

Hanson recoiled at the speech, stung by the reprimand.

"Do as you like," he said, his tone bitter.

Luther Corbett cut branches and improved the size and condition of Bear Le Vrette's lean-to. The marshal gathered up firewood and made the fire bigger. Hanson, with nothing else to do but become agreeable, led the horses down to a creek of snow melt running through the rocks.

"Two years ago, maybe three, I was up on this mountain with Bear Le Vrette," Luther said to the marshal as they worked to prepare for nightfall. "It was late fall and we was both hunting venison to get us through the winter. An early snow came through, and it was a vicious surprise. Up top you could not see to move. Down below the snow was bad enough. We was caught, both of us, away from our homes. Bear took me to a cabin he knew about. He never did say, but I came to believe, the way he picked through the cabin and touched some of the things there, that he had lived in that cabin at one time. I believe it was his cabin years before."

The marshal listened with interest. "You think that's where he's bound?"

Luther spat tobacco juice into the ground. "Bear didn't talk much about it, but I know he was married once and that his wife died. As I said, he didn't say much about it, but standing here now, I wonder if maybe that cabin he took me to in that fall snow was the cabin where he lived with his wife."

"Can you find the way back there?" the marshal asked.

"I don't know the answer to that. Did you say that when Bear Le Vrette killed Coggins he mentioned the name Caroline?"

"That's right," the marshal said. "He was calling the Hanson girl Caroline."

"That was the name of Bear's wife. Caroline. I never did know her — she died before I came into the mountains — but Bear spoke of her from time to time. Caroline."

"Do you think he believes the Hanson girl is his wife?" the marshal asked.

"This past winter was a long winter, cooped up in the cabin most of the time. I managed okay, but I had Sally. Old Bear is alone, and you never know how a long cold winter can beat down a man who is on his own. It may be that he ain't thinking right."

Luther Corbett watched the orange flames lick higher on the marshal's fire, the same fire that had warmed Bear Le Vrette and the Hanson girl earlier in the day. He wondered if Bear had gotten too old and too alone in the mountains.

"We'll follow their tracks tomorrow, and I will think on his old cabin and whether or not I can find my way there again."

***

Seth Hanson's sore feelings did not abate as they built the shelter, gathered wood, and cooked their dinner. Through the supper, as they chewed jerky, Seth Hanson stared across the fire at Luther Corbett, and there was a hatred in his eyes.

"You were a secesh, weren't you Corbett?" Hanson asked.

"I was."

"I was a Union man."

"I figured so," Luther Corbett said.

"How'd you figure that?" Hanson asked.

"You sound like a Midwesterner," Corbett said. "You're a farmer down in the valley. I just figured on you being in the Unioin army. Is that why you don't like me?"

"I don't like you because that man Bear Le Vrette who took my daughter is your people. Is he not your friend?"

"Bear Le Vrette is my friend," Luther Corbett said.

"Yes, exactly," Seth Hanson said, as if he had won a battle. "Like you, he is a mountain hermit, a trapper unfit to live among decent people. I believe the only reason you are here is to see that his life is spared. Admit it. Why are you here, Luther Corbett?"

"I am here because you and the marshal bade me here," Luther said. "I am here to help you in securing the return of your daughter. But you sought my help because Bear Le Vrette is my friend. So do not now complain to me about my choice of friends."

"My complaint with you is that I am not sure you're even helping us," Hanson said. "How do we know you're even telling the truth when you tell us we're on the right track?"

"I suppose you don't," Luther said.

Seth Hanson's fury boiled inside him. He could not endure the thoughts in his mind of what that old mountain man was doing to his daughter. His rage exploded, and Luther Corbett was the target of his venom.

Without warning nor justification, Seth Hanson reached into the fire pit and took hold of a thick branch that was only half in the fire. Hanson lifted the branch from the fire and in two quick strides was coming at Luther. Luther jumped to his feet and braced himself as Seth Hanson took a swing with the branch, and the lit end hit Luther in the shoulder in a burst of sparks.

"Hang on!" the marshal shouted, but his plea came too late. Having been struck, Luther defended himself. He dropped his shoulders and spread his arms and in a leaping tackle brought Seth Hanson to the ground, and they wrestled there, bumping into cedar branches, dead stumps and other debris. First one had the upper hand, and then the other.

Both men were strong from years of toil, and they fought like rams. They came off the ground and swung fists at each other, though hampered by heavy coats, all of the blows were to the shoulders and arms and caused little more than bruises.

The marshal tried to separate them, pulling on one and then the other. A mutual hatred had grown between the men, and they were not to be separated easily.

At last, exhaustion and the cold and heavy breathing in the high altitude quieted the violence between them, and they allowed themselves to be separated by the marshal.

"Now that's enough of that," the marshal said. "That's just enough. This won't help us bring back the girl. This won't help us stop Old Bear. That the two of you don't care for each other is plenty plain to see, but we ain't here for the two of you to care for each other. We're here for a purpose, and fighting between you won't serve that purpose. So enough of this."

Seth Hanson was breathing hard, but he had no heart to continue the fight. His rage, though, was not subdued.

"If we reach my daughter and find that she is beyond salvation because you have stalled us, I will kill you, Luther Corbett," Hanson said.

"Now, Seth, I said that's enough of this," the marshal said, and he had his arms spread wide and a hand on each man. "Enough, now."

CHAPTER 7

Old Bear Le Vrette knew this mountain well enough to keep going. He shifted around the supplies on the mules and put the girl on the back of one of the mules. If men were following him, and he believed they were, he might have made a mistake by leaving the shelter and the fire earlier in the afternoon. He had gone to pains to hide their trail, but when the rain let up and he decided to leave the afternoon shelter, Bear didn't do anything to break it down or hide it. He even left the few sticks in the fire to just burn themselves out. With night coming on now, Bear Le Vrette was thinking that had been a mistake. And so he figured if he'd left a track for men to follow the least he could do now is keep moving and extend the distance.

"We'll be home soon enough, Caroline," he told the girl. She looked feeble, worse than she had even before they stopped for the rain. She seemed weak and exhausted, and a couple of times she had emptied her stomach, throwing up on the side of the path. She needed warmth and food and water. But just now, Bear Le Vrette needed to keep moving, to get away from the men who were chasing him and Caroline. He could not remember who was chasing him, or why.

"Ain't many men could follow us," Bear said to the girl, though she was barely conscious, her head lolling as the mule bounced her along in the dark.

Le Vrette had to move slow. There was no light to see by other than the little bit of moonlight that could drift through the trees. But he knew this mountain. He knew the way the trail dropped down at an easy slope, following the creek that rushed along with the snow melt swelling its banks. In fact, up here, the creek really didn't even have banks, just a rocky bottom where the excess water pooled up on flat spaces before falling down its rocky trail and snaking through the level spots. Down below, the terrain evened out a bit and there were two big pools, mountain lakes, and when those were full — as they would be now — the water would spill down and rapid and twisting course in a more defined bed, cut away from the rocks over centuries. Another creek would join it a bit farther down, and there it became a river, and the river had cut a gorge down toward the valley, a deep gorge where Bear would find his first mountain cabin.

Here was where Bear and Caroline had made their home when they first came into the mountains, and it was here where they could make their home again now.

There by the gorge only one man knew the way in and out, and that man was Bear Le Vrette. The path that allowed him to get his mules to the small stable was too narrow and too tricky for any other mountain man. No one would now follow.

Bear wondered who it could be chasing behind him. Not many men could feel so at home in the mountains.

"Luther Corbett knows his way in the mountains," Bear said out loud, but the girl on the mule did not answer. "Luther is a good mountain man. He's learned quite a bit in the time he's been up here. Yes, I reckon young Luther could track us. But d'ye suppose he would? He has been a friend to me, but even your friends can turn to enemies after a long winter."

Lilly Grace moaned from atop the mule. "Mister, I can't go no further," she said, and her voice was slight.

"We've got to keep going, Caroline," Bear said. But all the same, he stopped walking and held the mule's lead rope. He reached up a hand and felt the girl's face. "You're burning up," Bear said. "My Lord, Caroline, you are on fire."

"From where will my help come?" Lilly Grace prayed. And then she said, "My help must come from thee." Bear Le Vrette thought the words were sung like a hymn, but he did not know any hymns.

Old Bear knew he must stop for the girl, but he feared if he stopped that the men pursuing would catch him.

He pushed on for a bit longer. He knew of a meadow not terribly far where they could make a stop and the mules would find grass and weeds to eat. When they at last reached the meadow, the girl was so faint that Old Bear had to lift her off the mule and lay her down on a bearskin while he made up a fire. It was slow going in the dark, but eventually he got the fire built. He made the fire at the edge of the meadow under a tree, and he used that tree to build a lean-to, and he pulled the girl under the shelter of the lean-to.

"You stay with me Caroline," Old Bear said to her. "I'll have you feeling better in no time."

He took a burning log from the fire to use as a torch so that he had light to see a little bit, and he sniffed out a white pine tree not far from the meadow. He gathered up a large fistful of fresh needles from the pine tree and used those to make a tea for the girl.

When the tea was good and hot, he poured some in a cup and then crawled under the lean-to with her.

"Come on, Caroline, drink this up. Ain't nothing like a good pine tea to revive you."

Old Bear sat under the lean-to and lifted the girl up so that she was sitting in his lap. Le Vrette tenderly held the girl's head against his chest and gently fed her some of the tea. He held her tiny body against him and vigorously rubbed her arms and shoulders.

"You've been so sick," he said. "You need to get your strength back, Caroline, if we're going to make it to the cabin."

After a time, the girl seemed to perk up a bit. The drink was hot and warmed her on the inside, and it was tangy and seemed to help to settle her stomach. As cruel as he was, Lilly Grace took comfort in the warmth of being cradled by the old man.

"May I have some more of the tea?" she asked.

Bear smiled to see her feeling improved.

"You certainly may," he said, and he went out to fetch more pine needles.

Bear made up another batch of the tea. The fire at the edge of the lean-to put off a smoke that clung in the top of the makeshift shelter, but it was warm inside the lean-to.

"The old cabin is going to need some fixing up,"

Bear admitted. "But in a week or two, I can have it back to being just like it was. And you know what a pretty spot it is, looking down over the gorge with the valley below and the peaks off in the distance. You used to always say it was the sweetest spot that ever God made."

Bear thought of the old cabin. It set back on a ledge away from the gorge with a small meadow where he kept his livestock. From the lip of the gorge, it was all rock straight down thirty feet to the narrow, rushing river, and straight back up another ten feet on the opposite side. Beyond the gorge was a small growth of tall Ponderosa Pines and spruce trees, but they did not block the cabin's view of the valley, stretching on for what seemed like a hundred miles. And beyond, on the far side of the valley going up the slope of the opposite peak, what an enormous stand of aspen that melted into a huge forest of spruce trees, and in the autumn the bright gold of the aspen and the dark green of the spruce and the slate gray of the mountain top and the white of the snow cap made it the most gorgeous view any man or woman had ever seen, and Old Bear and Carolina Le Vrette had spent many a day just sitting and looking at their view and marveling that God would have made that just for the two of them.

"It will be autumn again in a few months, Caroline," Bear said to the girl.

Lilly Grace felt too weak to argue, and she did not want to enrage the man.

Not far away she could hear water running through a creek in the woods. The water was running fast over rocks, and in her mind she could see it all frothy. It sounded like the creek that ran near her family's farm, and it made her sad to wonder if she would ever see that creek where she played with her brother.

When morning came, Lilly Grace woke with a start. She expected the old man to be there, laying atop her so that she could not get away. But the little lean-to was empty. She looked out into the meadow and did not see the man.

The fire was burning pretty well. He had put fresh branches on it not long ago for they were still putting off flames.

Lilly Grace gathered up the bearskin she had been wearing as a coat and held it over her shoulders as she peered out of the lean-to. The three mules, unburdened, were munching on the wildflowers in the meadow. The old man was not in sight anywhere.

Tentatively, Lilly Grace called out in a soft voice. "Hello? Mister? Are you there?"

She listened for a response, but none came.

Dawn was still gray, and Lilly Grace knew it must still be very early in the morning. She wondered where the man might have gone. She was scared to try, and she did not know where she would go, but Lilly Grace Hanson was determined. She stood up out of the lean-to. Her head swam. She was still sick and weak, though she felt better than she had the night before. She held on to the trunk of the tree to keep herself upright for a moment. And when her head leveled out and she believed she could take a step, Lilly Grace put first one foot and then the next into the woods. She did not see a trail, exactly, but she found the gentle upward slope that would take her higher, back the way she'd come.

She did not see the man, nor did she hear him. Now

was when she could escape.

One step and then the next. Move one foot and then the other. With one hand she held the bearskin over her, and with the other hand she braced herself on branches and tree trunks. One more step was another step closer to safety. Though she was going at such a terribly slow pace, the woods seemed to dash by in a blur. One step and then another. Another step and then one more. She just kept walking.

The ground below her feet seemed to get steeper. Lilly Grace prayed in her mind that God would deliver her safely to her home. One step and then another.

Bear Le Vrette stepped out from behind the bushy branches of a spruce tree, and he was not a foot in front of Lilly Grace. His enormous gray beard and dangerous eyes seemed to appear in front of her by some evil spell, and Lilly Grace screamed at the suddenness of his appearance.

"Where in tarnation do you think you are going?" Bear Le Vrette asked, and his voice was a rage, though not a shout.

"Please," Lilly Grace begged, "I just want to go home."

The back of Bear Le Vrette's hand smashed into Lilly Grace's cheek with such force that it knocked her to the ground. She let out of a cry of surprise and pain, and tears ran down her hot, throbbing cheek.

"Do not do that again, Caroline," Bear said. "You rile me so, and for no reason. I don't take pleasure in striking you. If you go running off like that, you will die on this mountain. Don't you see that? I cannot keep you safe if you won't stay with me."

"Please, I just want to go home," Lilly Grace said.

Bear Le Vrette reached down and dragged her up from the ground. "We are going home."

CHAPTER 8

What worried Luther Corbett were the sodden pine needles. White pine tea was an old Ute remedy. It helped to revive folks who were feeling sickly. If Bear Le Vrette had made up this tea for the girl, it meant she was sick. He wondered whether or not to share the information with the marshal and Hanson. Hanson would insist that they push harder. Luther held his hand over the coals of the fire.

"They lingered here this morning," Luther said. "The ashes here are still warm. Looks like they ate squirrel and brewed some tea. I would not think they started out more than a couple of hours ago."

"We're catching up to them," the marshal said. "Do you know which way they went?"

Luther looked out across the meadow. With the thick growth in the meadow, it was hard to find tracks. The mules had obviously been turned loose and nibbled at plants all across the meadow during the night and early morning.

Luther tried to remember the way Bear Le Vrette took him to the cabin a couple of years ago. Everything was all covered over in snow that time, and so it looked completely different.

"What I remember is the creek," Luther said. "I remember hearing the creek the entire way, and the cabin was in a meadow with the gorge created by the creek down below it. So long as we follow the creek, we should find them."

The creek cut down through the trees, not across the meadow, and so Hanson did not wait any longer. Hearing that they would follow the creek, he set off on his own.

"He's worried over his daughter," the marshal said to Corbett. "You understand that. I've known Seth Hanson just about as long as he's been out here in the territory. He's a good man, and I know he appreciates you tracking Old Bear and the girl. He's just worried, is all."

Corbett shrugged. "It don't hurt my feelings, none, marshal. I can sleep well at night whether Seth Hanson cares for me or not."

They could not ride fast, but the men stayed mounted as the descended down toward the valley, following the flowing water in the creek bed. At length, the creek pooled at the top of a ledge and then flowed off the ledge and dropped straight down into a deep gorge where it then continued its journey toward the valley floor. Luther stopped here for some time, looking out across the gorge and the lay of the land all around.

"We should go back up and find a crossing," Luther said. "We'll be on the wrong side of the gorge if we keep going down here."

Hanson complained that Luther should have said something and that backtracking would only waste more time. But there was no choice and then men climbed back a ways before finding a good crossing where they could safely walk their horses over and through the rapidly gushing stream.

As the creek cut a gorge down below them, the men were forced to walk their horses over a narrow ledge. Now that he was back here, Corbett remembered how harrowing this ledge had been when it was covered in snow. Bear Le Vrette assured him they would safely traverse the path, but Luther Corbett was nervous all the same. At that time the two men were snowed in together for five days. The cabin, not having been occupied for a number of years, was in disrepair and did little to keep the cold out, but Bear had left the cabin with a good supply of firewood, and the cabin proved to be a successful place for them to last out the early blizzard. When the weather broke and it warmed up again and the sun came back out, the two men made their way back across the mountains and valleys to their own homes. They had been careless that time. They had come too far for a hunt. There was plenty venison to be had in their own valleys. But Luther Corbett found that it was easy for a man up in the mountains to start to wander and then forget to stop, and this had been one of those times.

The men who came into the mountains a generation before Luther Corbett were rough and dangerous men. They drank heavily, they faced any danger, and many of them lived short lives. Old Bear Le Vrette had been one of these men. He'd known the old fur traders and trapped and hunted with them, men whose names had become legendary on the Oregon Trail and the California Trail.

The marshal and Hanson were a new breed of white men coming into the mountains. With them were men like them. Miners who sought gold and silver from the rock faces and river bottoms. Gamblers who sought gold and silver from the saloon parlors. Thieves and outlaws who sought gold and silver from other men's pockets. Farmers who sought to dig a livelihood out of the soil.

Luther Corbett fit with none of these men. He was a soldier who wanted to escape war, and the only way he could think to do it was to get as far away from other men as he could.

Now men from down below had come up and found him, and they had dragged him back into their troubles.

The rocky face that created the narrow path abruptly ended, and they found themselves out on a wide plateau thick with spruce trees.

"We're very close," Luther said, leading his horse to a small clearing. "If I remember it right, about three hundred yards through these trees is the clearing where Old Bear's cabin was."

The marshal looked through the trees, but there was nothing to see. "You wait here," he told Luther. "Be best for us to go in there and handle Le Vrette on our own."

Though he had brought them here, the marshal and Hanson still did not trust Luther Corbett, and that suited Luther just fine. He did not intend to pick up his rifle and kill his old friend, though Luther understood well that these men would not hesitate to do it.

From the small clearing there was a clear path, overgrown though it was with wildflowers and weeds.

Luther held the horses and the marshal and Hanson proceeded down the path.

Luther Corbett had a pit in his stomach, wondering how soon he would hear the snap and pop of rifles. He wondered if Old Bear would put up a fight. He wondered why Bear Le Vrette had taken this girl and what he intended to do with her.

Luther tied the three horses, took his rifle from its scabbard, and began walking along the path to get nearer. If there was an opportunity to intervene to save Bear Le Vrette's life, Luther Corbett intended to do it.

As he pushed his way through the thick growth of spruce trees and the tangle of weeds and wildflowers along the path, Luther could just see Hanson making his way up ahead. As Luther took another step, a branch protruding out into the path caught his eye. The branch had been shaved of twigs, and it was sticking into the path in an unusual way. As he followed the branch, he realized that it was a trigger, and a windlass with a kill stick had been wound between the trunks of two trees beside the path. At the top end of the kill stick a knife had been lashed to the stick like a spear blade.

Many years ago, Old Bear Le Vrette taught Luther Corbett how to make a windlass trap for catching small game.

Luther stepped back out of the way and picked up a large stone that he tossed onto the trigger stick. With shocking speed, the trigger sprung, and the kill stick dropped with amazing force. It was naught but chance that neither the marshal nor Seth Hanson had brushed by the trigger and set off the windlass trap. Old Bear had said the trap could be scaled bigger for killing bobcats and even bear, but Luther had only ever used a windlass for killing varmints. As he thought back to the day that Old Bear taught him how to make a windlass trap, Luther never expected to see the trap made to kill a man, but here it was.

Luther started to call out to the marshal and Hanson to warn them that Old Bear had set traps around the cabin, but he heard the clang of springing metal and knew instantly that his warning would come too late. Picking his step carefully, Luther Corbett hurried forward down the trail toward where he heard the marshal blaspheming loudly.

The marshal was on the ground, gasping for breath through gritted teeth. An iron bear trap was closed around his left leg. The marshal's face was pale as a snow cap.

"Try not to move it too much," Luther said. "Is the ankle broke?"

"May be," the marshal said, catching his breath as a wave of pain hit him. Luther examined the wound. One of the teeth of the clamp had dug in pretty good to the marshal's leg. Luther knew whether the ankle was broken or not, it would be days or weeks before the marshal would be fit to walk again.

Seth Hanson came up now.

"Watch where you step," Luther said. "Bear has set traps all through here."

Luther stepped down on one side of the trap to force the iron spring down, and Hanson stepped on the other side, but they could get no leverage to open the trap off the marshal's leg.

"We need trap clamps," Luther said.

The marshal sucked air, breathing heavy. "Damnation but it hurts," he said. "It was up under all these weeds and I never did see it."

"Where can we get clamps?" Seth Hanson asked.

Luther looked ahead toward Bear's cabin. "I reckon Bear Le Vrette has clamps. I have to wonder, though, if he'd be willing to loan them to us."

The marshal winced. "Sure would be good if we could get this off my leg."

"Hang tight, there marshal," Corbett said. He went back to the windlass trap he'd sprung and used his knife to cut the rope it was bound with. He took the rope back to the marshal and tied pieces on either side of the spring necks on first one side, then the other, of the trap. Luther then took a sturdy stick, not overly long so that he could turn it without bumping the marshal's bad leg too much, and he stuck a stick through one of the rope loops and began to wind the stick so that it would start to close the trap spring.

The marshal had to stand on his one good leg, and he support himself leaning against Hanson. Hanson stepped down on the spring arm to add his weight to the effort.

Corbett repeated the effort on the other side of the spring.

With the spring necks so clamped, Corbett grabbed either side of the trap jaws and forced them open, holding them down against the spring.

The marshal slid his mangled leg out of the trap, and when Corbett release the trap the ropes gave way and the trap sprung shut again.

"Lord, God Almighty," the marshal swore, laying back down in the weeds.

Luther examined the marshal's injured ankle. It was severe, and Luther knew that the marshal's survival was in doubt. If the bone was splintered the leg would have to be amputated. The marshal might easily get blood poisoning from where the iron tooth had bit into his leg.

"This is a bad situation," Luther said. "We need to get the marshal down to a town where a doctor can take proper care of him."

"We've got to go and get my daughter," Seth Hanson said.

The marshal's head was laid back in the weeds. His breathing was coming easier, but the man was still in awful pain.

"Go on and get the girl," the marshal said.

Hanson grabbed up his rifle and started toward the cabin.

"You'll want to watch where you step, Mr. Hanson," Luther said. "You might let me go first."

Hanson's face was red with anger. His lack of trust in Old Bear's friend was palpable.

"You've been fighting me the whole way," Luther Corbett said. "You've questioned every bit of advice I've offered, and this is after you and the marshal rode up to my cabin to ask me for help. And yet, I've led you to the man's door. Now you can go on, Mr. Hanson, or you can let me go first. It don't matter to me one way or t'other. I've done my part."

Hanson looked at the crippled marshal on the

ground.

"For Christ's sake, Seth, let the man lead the way," the marshal said.

Hanson stepped back away from the path, and Luther started forward.

The last obstacle in the way was a simple pit trap — a shallow hole with pointed sticks stuck into the side of it and covered over with weeds and wildflowers to make it look like the rest of the overgrown path. Luther spotted it easily when he saw the fresh dirt from the hole scattered about under the trees. He might have stuck a foot in the hole if he'd not been looking for it, but the lack of effort in the pitfall trap suggested to Luther that Old Bear Le Vrette's sloppy work was done in haste. Luther pulled the vines and weeds away to expose the hole.

The path opened up to a clearing where Le Vrette's cabin was snuggled up against some tall spruce trees on the opposite side of the clearing. A small stable with a corral was also in the clearing, and the corral was rich in tall grass and wildflower. Le Vrette's three mules grazed in the overgrown corral.

"He's here," Hanson said.

"Looks that way. Those are Old Bear's mules."

The stable was in decent shape, but the old house was in poor repair. A large spruce had fallen at the back corner and caved in the roof in the back. The tin-lined down spout was busted and knocked down, and the rain barrel at the back of the house was in pieces where the spruce tree had rolled off the house and smashed it. The mud between the logs meant to insulate was all washed away leaving wide gaps in the walls of the cabin. The doorway leading into the cabin was a gaping hole. Luther remembered them nailing up a bearskin when they weathered the snow storm here a couple of years ago, but that skin was gone now. Nothing could be seen through the open door, not at this distance.

"Even if he ain't looking for us, there ain't no way he won't see us coming," Luther said.

"Then we'll rush it," Hanson said.

Luther Corbett did not think that was a good idea, but at this point he chose not to offer any more suggestions.

"Will you help me?" Hanson asked.

"I'll not," Luther said. "If you choose to rush that cabin, I'll make no argument against it. But Old Bear's behavior perplexes me, and I am afraid that if he sees us coming he might do harm to the girl."

"So what would you recommend?" Hanson asked.

"Perhaps if you let me try to call him out. A scared animal backed into a corner is bound to bite. If we rush that cabin, Old Bear is going to feel like he's been backed into a corner. Maybe he shoots at us. Maybe he does harm to the girl. But if I can make him feel safe, like he has naught to fear and we just want to talk, then maybe he'll come out and we can end this."

Hanson looked at the cabin and thought of his daughter. . "Call to him, then."

CHAPTER 9

"Bear Le Vrette! Would you come out and have a word?"

Old Bear recognized Luther Corbett's voice, and it confirmed what he'd suspected. Luther Corbett was among the men tracking him.

"Please, mister," the girl said. "Please, let's just talk to them."

Bear Le Vrette's eyes were angry as he turned to look at the child. "You hush up now, and get up that rock. I'll brook no more insolence from you."

They were scaling the mountain wall behind the old, busted up cabin. The mountain rose up steep behind the cabin, in some places it was a straight rock face, but intermingled among the rocks were slopes with stands of spruce and pine. It was hard going up the slope, but not impossible. And the men tracking them would not be inclined to see them among the trees. So long as they stayed off the exposed rock, Bear believed they could summit the steep hill and then quickly put distance between them and their pursuers.

Bear had also heard one of the men hollering and knew that one of his traps must have worked. It was the hollering that alerted him, and he quickly grabbed Caroline by the wrist and started her up the steep slope.

He had only his rifle and a possibles bag filled with his powder horn, some lead balls, some jerky and other sundries that would help them. In his belt he had knife and hatchet.

"Caroline, girl, you've got to keep moving," Bear said impatiently. "These men will catch us up if you do not quicken your step."

"I am so weak," the girl complained. "I don't know how I can keep going."

"Luther Corbett is a smart man, and he knows his way in these mountains. If we're to escape them, we'll have to move faster now."

"I'm so tired and feel so ill," Lilly Grace said.

Bear Le Vrette was an old man, but he was built strong. He lifted the slight girl and put her over his shoulder, and though he breathed heavy they started to climb the slope at a faster pace. He grabbed hold to tree branches with one hand and pulled his weight as he took big steps to get higher up the slope. Still, behind him, he could hear Luther Corbett call out again.

"Bear Le Vrette! Come out of the cabin and let us have a word!"

Old Bear wanted to get to the top of the summit before Luther and whoever else was down there with him discovered that they had fled the cabin.

Lilly Grace thought each step would shake the life out of her. She seemed to bounce on the old man's shoulder. She wanted to call out to the men below, but she was too afraid to make a noise. So she bit her lip and said nothing as the man roughly scaled the slope of the mountainside. He seemed so large the way he lifted her over his shoulder, and Bear Le Vrette made Lilly Grace feel small.

But she was not helpless. She knew now that men, probably her father among them, were coming. And she prayed silently as the old man carried her, and as they went, she reached out and took hold of small branches and snapped them or stripped the needles and sprinkled them on the ground below. What Lilly Grace knew was that men were following, and she had to help them find her.

CHAPTER 10

"He ain't coming out," Seth Hanson said. "He ain't going to talk."

Luther was kneeling down and trying to peer across the clearing into the open doorway of the cabin. He could see nothing inside. The mules were in the corral. He didn't think Old Bear would have tried to trek without the mules, but Luther had to concede that it was possible Old Bear and the girl were not in the cabin.

"I reckon you're correct," Luther said. He was disappointed. He'd hoped Bear Le Vrette would see reason and turn loose the girl.

"I'm going in there now," Hanson said.

Luther clutched his rifle. "I suspect that's what we've got to do. Better let me go first. Old Bear's a good shot. If he's in there with his rifle pointed at us, he might not be so quick to shoot me."

He said it, but he didn't know if he believed it. Setting the traps along the path to the cabin had been a

71

dastardly thing, and Luther Corbett's opinion of his friend was diminished by the act. He believed now that Old Bear might shoot him just as quick as he'd shoot the others. But he somehow felt a responsibility for the friendship, and if Old Bear was going to shoot at somebody, Luther thought it was his place to be the one.

Seth Hanson followed Luther out into the clearing. Luther walked deliberately, watching the ground in front of him for signs of traps and also watching for movement or a gun barrel or any sign of life from the cabin. The fear he had was that maybe Old Bear had killed the girl and Hanson was about to discover the body of his dead daughter. It was a frightful thought.

As they came upon the cabin door, Luther stepped inside.

"Empty," he said. "They ain't in here."

Luther Corbett made a quick look around. He rifled through the baggage that had come off the mules. "They left out of here in a hurry," Luther said. "Old Bear's left just about everything. I don't see his powder horn or rifle. Looks like he took his hatchet and knife. I don't see his possibles bag. But he didn't take much else."

Seth Hanson dashed out of the cabin and started looking around.

"Lilly Grace!" Hanson called out, cupping his hands to his mouth to project his voice. "Lilly Grace Hanson! Can you hear me?"

Seth Hanson listened as his own voice echoed off the distant mountains, but he heard no reply from his daughter.

Luther walked out of the cabin carrying an Indian

blanket he'd taken from Bear's packs.

"Which way did they go?" Hanson asked. "Can you find some sign of them?"

"We need to see to the marshal," Luther said. "We need to see to the marshal and get the horses into the corral. We'll start after them when we've done these things."

Luther cut a couple of branches and made a travois, and the two men helped the marshal to lay down on that. Together, they dragged it along the path, lifting it over the pit trap, and across the clearing to Bear Le Vrette's old cabin. They beat the dust off an old bear rug that was in the cabin and laid that down on Bear's cot, and they helped the marshal onto the cot. The man was in tremendous pain, but he did not complain much.

Luther went to get the horses from where he'd tied them and brought them into the corral. With Hanson, they unsaddled the horses and let them roam with the mules. Hanson took a canteen to the marshal and did what he could to bandage the wound, though the slightest touch caused the marshal pain.

The corral was fenced in by just an old snake fence, and about half the rails were knocked down. Luther went along and picked them up and remade the fence as best he could, though some of the rails were rotting from where they'd sat in the damp for too long. He just needed it to be good enough to hold for now.

When the fence was finished, Luther got some of the old stacked logs and made up a fire in the cabin. The stone fireplace and chimney were still intact.

"We should be getting on if we're going to catch

them," Hanson said.

"I'm aware," Luther told him. "But we've got to get the marshal set up here. He'll not survive if we can't get some food in him and get his strength up. His leg is in bad shape."

"Go on and get moving," the marshal said from the cot. "I'll be fine. Sooner you get to the girl, the sooner you can get back to me."

Luther rinsed out an old pot he found among Bear Le Vrette's packs and dropped some of the pemmican into it with water.

"Heat up this stew and give it to him," Luther told Hanson. "I'm going to see if I can pick up some sign of their trail."

It was already getting late in the day, and Luther knew if he didn't find a trail soon they would have to spend the night in the cabin. But he was growing worried for the girl. He did not know what condition she was in, and now that Bear was traveling without supplies, Luther was worried that the girl's health would suffer.

Bear had lived in this cabin and would know the best route of escape. When Old Bear first lived here the Indians, Ute and Arapaho, sometimes threatened miners and trappers. He would have had a plan if hostile Indians happened upon the cabin.

Luther Corbett looked out across the terrain to figure how Old Bear Le Vrette might have gotten away. If he dropped down, following the creek, the going was tough that way. Luther could see there was not just a steep slope, but it was rocky and craggy and would be slow going. Obviously Bear had not followed the creek back upstream, because that would have brought him face to face with his pursuers. Luther examined the gorge, but there was no place where Bear and the girl might have crossed — no felled tree or narrow gap — nor was there a way for them to descend down into the gorge.

The only option was for Bear to have scaled the slope behind the cabin.

Luther took a long look up toward the summit. At first glance, it didn't look a likely route. There were many large rock faces that would have been difficult, if not impossible, to scale. But Luther could trace a route that would have allowed Bear and the girl to mount the slope entirely hidden by the tall and thick spruce trees. It would have been a journey with many switchbacks that would have taken them first one way and then the other as the rock faces jutted out in the middle of the spruce forests, but Luther could see the way.

Luther walked to the door of the cabin.

"We should go now," he said to Hanson. "Marshal, we'll be back for you as quick as we can. It likely won't be before tomorrow. Stay warm. Eat that stew and drink water. Keep wood on the fire. Don't move around more than you have to, and don't try to put weight on that bad ankle. I wish there was more we could do for you."

Hanson did not hesitate. He took up a bag and put some jerky in it, as well as cartridges for his rifle.

"Take my Colt," the marshal said to Luther. "You might need it."

Luther did not argue. He took the weapon and the marshal's holster.

As the two men started to leave the cabin, the

marshal called to Seth Hanson.

"Seth, if you want to get your daughter back, you do what Luther tells you to do. He has been true to us to get us this far. You'll have to trust him to help you finish this."

Luther spat tobacco juice into the grass outside the cabin.

They took only the barest of essentials — some jerky, hatchets, knives, and guns, their blankets rolled and wrapped over a shoulder in a way that reminded Luther Corbett of going on march in the war. They would have to move quickly and catch Bear Le Vrette soon, or they might well fall victim to hunger or exposure.

There might have been half a dozen trails that Bear and the girl could have taken, but Luther followed his instincts for what seemed the most natural way to scale the slope. Here and there he back-tracked when the trail seemed to peter out on him. He looked back down the slope several times. Bear would not have taken any route that would have exposed him to people down below, and if Luther could see the cabin clearly, he knew he was off track.

They were well up the slope and breathing hard when Luther Corbett first noticed the broken spruce twigs. They were frequent enough that the trail was easy to follow. Luther picked up the pace though he was physically exhausted. When there was not a freshly broken twig within easy sight, he found limbs that were shaved of needles. Below these, he discovered the spruce needles scattered on the ground. It seemed the girl was leaving them an easy trail to follow.

Or maybe it was Old Bear. Luther didn't have to imagine hard to think that Old Bear might be leading them to a trap. But he doubted it. They were too close behind him. He wouldn't have time to do more than he'd already done. And his traps had been with the packs in the cabin.

"You're going too fast," Hanson said. "How can you be sure you're going the right way?"

Luther stopped to catch his breath. Hanson, too, was grateful for the break.

"Your daughter is a smart girl," Luther said. He took a few steps to a spruce branch and bent it toward Seth Hanson. "Do you see this here?"

Hanson stepped closer. A twig on the branch was broken and formed a small triangle. The break was clearly fresh.

"Lilly Grace broke that?" Hanson asked.

"She must have. I've been following a trail of broken twigs for the last several minutes."

Luther let go of the branch and looked forward. He pointed up ahead. "See there? There's another. Somehow, she's breaking all these twigs, or skinning them of needles, and Old Bear doesn't know she's doing it. How long were we at the cabin caring for the marshal?"

Hanson shrugged. "Perhaps an hour. Maybe a quarter of an hour."

"Then I believe that's how far in front of us they are," Luther said. "And with this trail, we will gain on them fast. So long as your girl keeps breaking these twigs, we can have them before sundown.

CHAPTER 11

Bear Le Vrette discovered Lilly Grace's deception as he passed a spruce tree and felt it tug as he tried to move forward. The twig did not break clean, and Lilly Grace held on to it too long. Old Bear set the girl down on her feet and turned and looked at his back trail. He could see a half dozen broken twigs all along the route. The old mountain man flew into a rage, and he swung his hand across his body so that the back of his hand smashed into the girl's face.

Lilly Grace let out a whimper and shrank away from the old man covered in bearskin.

"What have you done?" he raged. "They'll follow us for sure, now."

"Just leave me here," Lilly Grace begged. "Just leave me and you keep going. You can get away, and when they find me I will tell them not to follow you."

"I'll never leave you, Caroline," Old Bear said. "We'll get out of this yet. And when we do, it'll be just like it was before."

She did not feel well, but she felt brave. The old man had struck her. He might do it again, but he would do no worse.

"I am not Caroline," Lilly Grace Hanson said defiantly. "My name is Lilly Grace, and you have me confused for someone else."

Old Bear Le Vrette looked at the girl for several moments, and for just a second, Lilly Grace felt bad for the sadness in his eyes. But then his eyes turned to fury again, and he took her by the shoulders and he shook her so hard that her brain seemed to rattle. "Don't you ever say that again," Bear commanded her. "Don't never talk like that again."

When Le Vrette turned loose of her, Lilly Grace fell to her knees, and she was crying violently again. But Old Bear paid no attention to her sobs. "What we have to do now is figure a way out. There's a way. We just have to figure it."

They had reached the summit of the hill some time before, and now they were going out across a long, wide ridge heavily covered in trees and big rocky outcroppings. Old Bear had been up here many times hunting goat and deer. But he had never attempted to flee pursuers up here, and that made it tricky to know how best to use the landscape to his advantage. The girl had complicated things with her deception, but escape was still not impossible. It would just take some deception of his own.

Bear reached down and took Lilly Grace roughly by the wrist and pulled her to her feet.

"No more tricks from you," he said.

Once again, he lifted her over his shoulder, and now

he carefully walked back the way he'd come for sixty yards or so. He picked his steps carefully, staying on the balls of his feet, to avoid leaving any tracks. Each time he spotted one of Lilly Grace's broken twigs, he got aggravated all over again.

At length he came to what he was looking for, a long stretch of bald rock with no trees or dirt. The bald rock gave him an opportunity to double back and then set out on a new path. With luck, Luther Corbett and whoever else was following would continue on down the initial path and never follow back here to the rock. The ridge eventually dropped down into the valley below. With luck, Luther would follow it all the way into the valley before realizing he had been deceived.

And that would give Old Bear the time he would need to circle back to the cabin, get his mules and supplies, and set off for a new destination, though Bear Le Vrette did not yet know what that new location would be.

Bear hurried out across the bald rock. He knew Luther was not terribly far behind him. The rock curved out for thirty yards or so before it abruptly ended and the big spruce forest continued. When Bear reached the tree line, he set Lilly Grace down.

"You'll walk from here," he said. "If you're strong enough to break twigs, you're strong enough to walk. And no more tricks from you."

Having found her voice, Lilly Grace was not ready to be silenced. As they pressed deeper in among the trees, she said to Bear, "Please just take me back and let me go."

"You don't know what you're saying," Bear argued. "You're weak from feeling poorly, and you're not talking sense."

"Was Caroline your wife?" Lilly Grace asked.

Bear Le Vrette reached out and grabbed her by the arm and squeezed hard against her muscle.

"You are my wife," he said. "You are my wife, Caroline."

Though she was young, she began to understand. "But surely you must realize I am too young to be your wife," Lilly Grace said.

"Stop talking," Bear said. "Just stop talking. You're aggravating me."

"You're confused," Lilly Grace said. "You're confused because you're lonely and you miss your wife. I understand that. I miss my family, too."

Again, the old man's eyes turned sad. "I have missed you for so long," he said, and his voice was different now. His voice sounded deeper, almost breathless. "The winter was so long without you. Do you not remember how we used to laugh? Do you not remember how you used to speak to me with such a tenderness to your voice? It took a different breed of woman to come up into these mountains with me. You warn't never like other women, Caroline."

"I feel so sad for you," Lilly Grace said. Tentatively, she reached out and touched the old man on the arm, an act of compassion he had not earned but she felt compelled to give. "But you have to realize that I am not Caroline. My name is Lilly Grace Hanson."

Lilly Grace saw the eyes flash, and she knew his mood was on the verge of turning sour again.

"I'm going," she said, and she started to walk again. She could feel the old man following her.

Lilly Grace did not realize it, but they had made a big loop through the spruce trees and were now back to the top of the slope overlooking the cabin. But the trees were so thick that she could not see the cabin, she could only tell that the elevation of the land was quickly dropping again.

As they descended the slope, Lilly Grace thought she could smell the familiar and comforting smell of a chimney fire.

Bear Le Vrette could smell it, too, and as he walked he loaded powder and ball into his old muzzle-loader rifle.

"Someone's down below," Bear said to the girl. "When we get there, I'll deal with whoever it is."

CHAPTER 12

"She stopped breaking twigs," Luther said. "I've not seen one in the last few minutes."

Hanson looked around, but he did not see a broken twig, either. "Maybe we've gone the wrong way."

Luther Corbett looked as far as he could see down the trail they'd been following. "I don't think so," Luther said. "We're on a natural trail, one animals use. Old Bear is looking to move quickly, and this is the best way for him to do that, following an existing trail like this. We could turn back, but I'm afraid we'd lose too much time. It's better to keep going. Maybe Old Bear caught her doing it and stopped her."

Seth Hanson tried not to think about the moment the old man caught his daughter breaking twigs. It pained him to consider that Bear might have been enraged and punished her.

The two men continued down the trail, dropping lower and lower toward the valley below.

Darkness was coming on fast as the sun began to slide down below the mountains, but Luther Corbett did not stop. He was greatly concerned that he had seen no sign in some time. The mules were good for leaving tracks to follow or at last an occasional sign that he was still moving in the right direction, but now that Bear Le Vrette was on foot without the mules, these occasional confirmations did not exist. Luther was certain Bear would have kept descending the trail, but he ached to see something to prove him right.

With the growing darkness, the mountain air was getting chilly. In among the trees and lower down the mountain, the wind was not so bad. But Seth Hanson was getting cold. "Should we stop for the night?" Hanson asked. Luther took a breath. He did not want to admit his mistake, but he was becoming increasingly convinced that he'd made a wrong decision.

"We might need to turn back," he said. "I am no longer convinced that they are on this trail. We might need to return to where we last saw the broken twigs and try to catch their path there."

Hanson flew into a rage. "But that was four, maybe five miles back! You said you were sure they'd come this way!"

Luther Corbett nodded. "I was certain. But now I am not certain. We should turn back. We can make up lost time in the dark. This trail is easy enough to follow. In the morning we'll search to pick up the trail again."

Hanson knew it would only waste time to argue, but as they turned back and began climbing the mountain again, he questioned Corbett.

"Are you sure we lost the trail? Are you sure they did not descend into the valley?"

"I am sure we lost the trail," Corbett said. "I am not sure they did not descend into the valley. I've seen no sign of them since the last of the broken twigs. I've seen no footprint, no broken branch, no mark in the dirt that would indicate someone sliding. I've seen nothing that tells me they came this way. I am afraid if we continue down the mountain without seeing some sign that we will have lost them completely. This is a troublesome moment," Corbett admitted. "If we go late into the morning and are still unable to pick up their trail, Bear Le Vrette could be very far indeed. If we find no sign of them tomorrow at all, then we might conclude that we will never find them."

"Never find them?" Hanson asked. "You cannot be serious."

"These mountains go on forever," Luther Corbett said. "A man could be lost up here his whole life. If we don't find their trail tomorrow, we might never find it, and the only hope we would have is to accidentally wander upon them."

Soon the sky was too dark and the woods so black that they had only the faintest of light from which to see. The temperature dropped severely, and Luther decided to stop and build a fire. It was difficult going in the dark just finding good wood to burn, and it took a long time for the fire to get going. Neither man had eaten in several hours, and they did not have much with them for nourishment now. They brought no coffee nor a pot to cook it in, so they drank water, unrolled their blankets and spent a cold, hungry night near the fire, both hoping that the light of dawn would point them in the right direction.

CHAPTER 13

The marshal could not sleep for the pain in his leg, but he was not altogether conscious, either, when he heard what he thought was Luther Corbett and Seth Hanson returning.

"Did you find them?" he called out through the tattered walls of the log cabin. He looked through the gaps and could see two people near the cabin, but he could not see enough to make out who it was. For a moment, his heart leapt as he realized one of the people outside the cabin was a young girl. But then the other person came on fast, and too late the marshal realized this person was wearing a bearskin coat — neither Luther Corbett nor Seth Hanson wore a bearskin coat — and the marshal knew what this must portend.

He reached for his rifle, propped beside the cot, but he could not get his hand on it fast enough. The old mountain man, who in that skin coat looked more bear than human, was filling the doorway to the cabin, and an ominous and threatening sight he made.

The marshal leaned to grasp the rifle, but Bear Le Vrette was on him too fast.

In the dim light of the cabin, Old Bear saw all he needed to see in an instant. A stranger in his cot with his leg bandaged and propped up. Bear understood, even before the scene registered as thoughts in his mind, that the traps he'd set had succeeded. He'd heard the man holler — that had alerted him so that he and Caroline could make their escape — and now here was the man, incapacitated.

Bear Le Vrette threw himself onto the marshal, knocking away the rifle before the marshal even had a good grasp on it. Bear drove his knee into the injured ankle, and the marshal vehemently exclaimed. Bear bashed the marshal's face with his big fists: three, four, five times he hit him.

Without mercy, Bear Le Vrette dragged the wounded marshal from the cot, allowing his busted leg to slide across the rough ground, sending waves of pain shooting through the dazed marshal. Out of the cabin and across the meadow the big man dragged the marshal. The marshal could offer little resistance. The pain in his leg, and now his face all busted by Bear Le Vrette's heavy fists. The marshal pushed against the big man, but Bear held him fast. They were going toward the ledge overlooking the gorge, and with horror the marshal realized that Bear Le Vrette intended to throw him over the side.

"No!" the marshal cried out, and with renewed strength he tried to swing at the big man's face or break Le Vrette's grasp on his shirt, but the marshal could not force himself free.

Bear Le Vrette dropped the marshal roughly to the rocky ground at the precipice.

"Never again will man nor beast separate me from my wife," Old Bear growled.

The marshal rolled and attempted to crawl away, but Bear Le Vrette stepped down hard against the marshal's shattered leg, and the lawman could do naught but cry out. Bear Le Vrette had his knife in his hands, and the marshal's eyes grew wide with horror as Bear Le Vrette stooped down over him and cut a deep gash across his throat.

Bear Le Vrette then took the marshal under his arms and carelessly tossed him from the ledge of the deep gorge, down to the rocky rapids of the river thirty-five feet below.

The horrific violence and the suddenness of it rooted Lilly Grace Hanson where she stood. If she had given thought to escape while Bear Le Vrette was occupied with the marshal, her thoughts evaporated when she witnessed the terrible way that Le Vrette dispatched the marshal.

"Get into the cabin," Le Vrette said, and his voice was thick with rage.

Lilly Grace ran to the cabin and fell to her knees in the corner where the spruce tree had smashed the roof. Debris was all around her and cut into her knees, but she paid it no heed. "Oh, dear Heavenly Father, please have mercy on the soul of that poor, ill-treated man," she implored, and her sobs came anew when she considered that the murdered man had been in the mountains to save her. She did not notice the marshal's rifle on the ground.

Bear Le Vrette considered the horses in his corral. He recognized the one as Luther Corbett's horse but did not know the other two horses.

Old Bear watched the slope above his old cabin for

a long time as the dying sun hit the rock faces. He watched for any movement, any shake of a tree, any slide of a rock, anything that might indicate the owners of the horses would be returning to the cabin this night.

With the shadow of the opposite mountain now upon him and not enough light to see, Old Bear decided he would not have visitors tonight. He believed his ruse must have worked and sent his pursuers well down the toward the valley in the wrong direction.

Bear walked back to the cabin where there was still a fire going. The girl was kneeling in a corner talking to herself.

"What are you doing there?" Bear asked angrily.

"I am praying for the soul of the man you killed," Lilly Grace told him.

"If a man don't want to die he should mind his own business." Bear found the packs his mules had carried still on the dirt floor of the cabin. "Stop that there and fix me up something for supper. There's pemmican there, and in that bag there are onions and potatoes. Fry it up over the fire."

Lilly Grace wanted to refuse. She wanted to argue and tell Old Bear Le Vrette that if he wanted his supper he could prepare it for himself. But she said nothing. Instead, she got together the pot and the food. She took a knife and cut the onion and potato.

Bear Le Vrette laid back on his cot, exhausted from so much moving. In the morning they would move again. Luther Corbett would not be fooled for long. Whether he realized that Bear had circled back to the cabin or merely intended to come back for his injured comrade, Bear knew that Luther Corbett and the other man would arrive at the cabin some time in the morning or early afternoon.

"They nearly had us today, Caroline," Old Bear said, but the girl did not respond. "We'll have to do better tomorrow."

With his mind wandering to the trails around the old cabin, those trails where he once hunted and trapped, Bear Le Vrette started to doze off. He did not intend to fall asleep, but exhaustion had overcome him.

Lilly Grace paid no mind to the old man while she fried the pemmican and vegetables until she heard him snort. Sparing a glance, she realized Bear Le Vrette was asleep. She quietly set the pot down on the dirt floor of the cabin and slowly, careful with each step, tiptoed from the cabin. Outside it was already starting to get cold. Lilly Grace hugged herself and shivered. She took a few tentative steps out into the meadow. One of the horses in the corral snorted.

It was too dark to see anything more than shadows, and Lilly Grace had no idea which way to go. At last she turned around and walked back into the cabin where she finished cooking the food.

CHAPTER 14

At first light Luther Corbett and Seth Hanson hurried back up the trail the way they'd come the previous afternoon. Luther felt tired and weak. He was accustomed to hard living on hunts and trapping expeditions, but pursuing a man was an entirely more difficult challenge. They were poorly supplied, too. Luther had thought he would be back home to his own cabin by now and had not prepared to be on the trail so long. And the necessity of haste meant there was no opportunity to hunt for food.

Worse than the exhaustion, Luther Corbett felt a responsibility for missing the trail the previous afternoon. They had lost hours, perhaps had lost the girl forever, because Luther had pressed forward though he had no sign. He was determined now to rectify his mistake and get back the Hanson girl.

It seemed an eternity to finally get back to a spot where they'd last seen the sign left by the girl.

"There, up ahead, is a broken twig," Seth Hanson said, hurrying forward.

All along the way Luther had kept a careful look either for sign he might have missed the previous afternoon or for a trail that Old Bear Le Vrette might have taken. But he'd seen nothing that was promising.

With the broken twig in sight again, Luther stopped on the trail and looked up and down it in every direction. He could see nothing that might suggest an alternate route, no sign at all that the girl and Le Vrette had come any farther than this spot where the broken twig was. Examining the ground below the last broken twig, Luther Corbett found what he had missed the previous day. Scars in the ground told of a tussle. The evidence did not suggest much of a fight, but clearly something had happened here. Imagining how the prints had been made, Luther concluded that the girl had been knocked to the ground. If Bear Le Vrette struck her, he must surely have realized that she was leaving a trail. So the question Luther Corbett had to answer was how Bear would disguise his tracks.

Luther looked around for some sign from the terrain.

"When we were coming up through here yesterday, did we not pass a large bald stone face? Perhaps not much farther along the path here."

Seth Hanson tried to remember. "Perhaps," he said. "I am not certain."

Luther Corbett thought he was certain. "That would be exactly the sort of place where a man could walk and leave no trail to follow," Luther said. "Not dirt to leave a track. No tree where branches or twigs my be broken. Just a wide, flat stone that a man might walk over a hundred times and never leave a trace. I am thinking that Old Bear discovered that your daughter was leaving a trail, and I believe when he realized this he decided to backtrack to that stone face. And there, I believe, he crossed freely without concern that we might pick up his track."

Luther had a terrible thought, but he did not voice it. Bear Le Vrette might well have decided to backtrack all the way to the cabin. And if he did this, he would have found the marshal hobbled and helpless.

The thought might have indicated a need to rush to the cabin, but Luther Corbett made up his mind. The marshal was a man who wore a badge. Lilly Grace Hanson was an innocent girl, abducted by a man who'd lost his mind. Luther was on this mountain to save the girl, and so he must track the girl.

They came to the bald rock and walked out across it. There would not be anything to see upon the rock, but the sign Luther sought was where Bear Le Vrette and the girl reentered the woods.

Luther was drawn to the path that seemed to most naturally take them back down toward the cabin. Here, where the rock turned back to dirt, the snow and rain had run off the rock and left mud, and here in the mud Luther found the tracks he was seeking.

"They've come this away," Luther Corbett called to Seth Hanson. "We should hurry."

Luther did not worry much for trying to follow tracks or seek out further sign. He knew, instinctively, that Bear Le Vrette had doubled back to the cabin. He feared what they found there would be awful.

Luther walked quickly through the woods, and Seth was breathless to keep up. But finally they came back to the ridge overlooking the cabin, and Seth Hanson recognized where they were.

"Isn't the old cabin down this way?" Seth asked.

"It is," Luther confirmed.

"You don't think they returned to the cabin?"

"I think that they did," Luther said.

"But what about the marshal?" Hanson asked.

"We will know soon," Luther said. "Either the marshal heard them coming and was ready for Bear Le Vrette, or Bear knew the marshal was in the cabin and got a jump on him. I reckon one of the two of them is dead."

The steep slope made going down as difficult as going up, but the men took the slope as fast as they could. There was still smoke curling up from the chimney.

"Bear Le Vrette may be in the cabin," Luther said as they neared the bottom of the slope. "We should approach the cabin with caution."

Even as he said it, Luther noticed that the mules were no longer in the corral, though the three horses were. That was a poor omen for the fate of the marshal.

With their rifles shouldered, the men slowly approached the cabin, but they found it empty. Bear's packs were gone, but so too was the marshal. The fire was close to burning out. It had not had new fuel since early in the morning.

"They've been here and left," Seth Hanson said.

"Surely."

"Did they take the marshal with them?"

Luther stepped out of the cabin into the meadow.

"They did not," he said.

"Then where is he?"

Luther looked over at the stable. He looked at the tall spruce and mountain pines beyond the meadow. He hoped to find the marshal alive and tied to a tree or bound in the stable, but he did not. "We will find him presently," Luther said.

Tentatively, determined not to find what he suspected would be there, Luther Corbett walked toward the ledge overlooking the gorge. He saw the stained dirt and suspected a murder had happened there at the precipice. He walked to the spot and looked down into the gorge, and there he saw the shattered body of the marshal, busted against the rocks below.

Seth Hanson came out to the ledge to where Luther was standing and looked over.

"Le Vrette killed the marshal," he said.

"He did," Luther acknowledged.

Seth Hanson was going to say something, but his voice was cut short with the sound of a thud. At the same moment that Hanson grabbed at his stomach, Luther heard the report of a filed musket. The gunshot echoed back and forth, and it was hard to determine where it came from. It took a moment, just a second or two, for Luther Corbett to realize that Seth Hanson was clutching his stomach and that blood was rapidly flowing in between his fingers.

Hanson wobbled and started to pitch forward toward the gorge, but Luther reached out and grabbed him and dragged him away.

Now Luther fully understood. Somewhere on the

opposite side of the gorge, Bear Le Vrette had fired a musket ball that punched Seth Hanson in the gut.

Luther half dragged, half carried Hanson all the way back to the cabin, and there he laid him down on the cot. He first pulled Hanson's hands away from the wound. He watched as the blood pooled on Hanson's torso and ·then flowed over.

"You're bleeding bad," Luther said. Using his knife, Luther cut the shirt away. He balled up the shirt and pushed the blanket onto the wound to compress it to stop the bleeding.

"I'm killed," Hanson said. He gritted his teeth and breathed in short, quick breaths. "A man doesn't survive a wound like this."

Luther had seen plenty of men gut shot like this in the war, and he didn't know many to survive. Even if he was able to slow the bleeding, the lead ball was buried somewhere inside Seth Hanson. Blood poisoning was likely. Luther had no way of getting the lead out of Hanson's stomach, he had no way of stopping the bleeding. Though he'd watched many a man get shot in the war, all he knew of treating bullet wounds was putting a man on a stretcher and carrying him to a hospital tent. Or, as was too often the case, sitting with him until he died. Luther Corbett figured this was a case of the latter as there were no hospital tents in the mountains.

"Hold this shirt against the wound," Luther said. "I'm going to get you bandaged up."

"No," Hanson said, and he reached out and took hold of Luther's shoulder, digging his fingertips into the man. "Promise me you will not quit. Promise me that you will continue to pursue Bear Le Vrette until you are able to rescue my daughter from him. And when you have her, take her home to her mother."

"I can't leave you to die here," Luther said.

"You can't stop me from dying here." Seth Hanson's words came slow, between labored breaths, but they were deliberate words "But what you can do is you can finish what we started. I did not trust you, Corbett. But you've proved me wrong. Like you said, without you, we'd have never got this far, never got this close to saving Lilly Grace. I've no right to ask it, other than upon the foundation of human decency, but I've also no other choice. So I'm asking you to go on now, alone, without me and without the marshal, and save my daughter. Will you make a dying man that promise?"

"I'll take the girl back to her mama," Luther Corbett swore. "And I'll come back for you."

"If you come back for me," Seth Hanson said, "you'll only come back to bury me."

"I'll come back," Luther said.

CHAPTER 15

Men who lived in the mountains did not take wives. They might keep a squaw, but white women did not come into the mountains. But Bear Le Vrette was an oddity.

He was in Saint Jo with a pile of furs he'd brought down first the Platte River and then the Missouri River. With him were other men of the trapping company. They had come so far to resupply, but mostly they came to trade beaver pelt and bearskin for whiskey and whores. Old Bear met Caroline in Saint Jo. She'd come this far with a husband who was now dead. Without means of returning east or going farther or supporting herself in anyway, she turned to whoring. But that was no life that she enjoyed. She liked Old Bear Le Vrette because he made her laugh. Drunk, he talked about the glory of the mountains and the hardness of the life there, and as he talked of it, Caroline wondered if the harsh winters could be worse than laying below drunken, smelling men night after night.

She asked Bear, and he did not have the will to refuse her. She had the prettiest blue eyes, blue like the sky on a crystal clear day.

"I do not think you'll survive the winter," he said. "Naught but Injun women can live among them mountains, and few of them can do it. But if you wish to come along and try it, I ain't going to say you cannot."

That was as close to a marriage vow as they ever shared, but when Caroline survived the first winter living with Bear in his cabin, they both took to thinking of each other as a spouse. Caroline survived by adopting the masculine mannerisms. She wore pants and shirts and boots like a man. She learned to trap and skin a beaver. She accepted the cruelties of the mountains and adored all the things that brought men here. The freedom. The beauty. The danger. Caroline adopted a lust for life she'd never known below, and her return visits to trading posts or towns were infrequent. She had a fondness for Bear Le Vrette, too, though he could be sour at times and was set in his ways. He treated her with a tenderness. Bear Le Vrette understood that Caroline was a treasure, one in a thousand or maybe one in ten thousand. No other man in the mountains had a woman unless she was a squaw.

Something like love blossomed between the two of them, and they lived together for several years in the mountains.

It did not matter how cold the winter got or how tough the beaver were to skin or how hungry they sometimes got when game was scarce, Caroline could always laugh, and her pretty eyes would light up and Bear Le Vrette was forced to wonder if he was not living the greatest life that any man had ever lived.

Sure, at times Caroline got surly, but it wasn't often. Bear only ever had to hit her a few times, and she always blamed it on his passions. And one fall he went off on a long hunt thinking he might not come back, but he did. But most of the time they shared a good life together.

After eight or ten years, or maybe it was a dozen, Caroline took ill one spring. She did not recover, and she died in the bed they shared in the cabin they had built together. She had helped to dig out the hard earth, had chopped and sawed the logs, had helped to lift them into place. Bear said she could do the work of two men.

When she passed, Bear buried her near the cabin and he left. He could not stand to go on in that place where they'd shared so many happy days now that all the joy had gone out of his world.

When he saw her bright blue eyes down at Coggins' trading post, Old Bear Le Vrette could not understand how she had come back to him, but all that mattered was that Caroline was returned.

He did not want to kill Luther Corbett. The other two men meant nothing to him. He hoped their deaths would serve as a warning to Luther. Old Bear liked Luther and admired the way he'd taken to trapping and hunting. Not every man could make his way in these mountains, but Luther turned out to be a good and smart man. Bear believed that the mountains helped to heal Luther of the viciousness of war. He warn't so callous as he'd been when he first come up. It seemed a shame to take that away from him, just as the man was starting to learn to breathe again.

But if Luther Corbett could not be dissuaded, he would have to be killed.

Bear put Caroline on the back of one of the mules as they descended down toward the valley. He did not now have a destination in mind. Luther's interfering had spoiled the cabin.

In the valley they would find sustenance. Meat would be more plentiful. Berries would be ripe. The need for shelter would not be so great in the valley where the air wasn't so cool and the wind did not whip quite as hard. They could better survive down below.

The afternoon thunderstorm that kicked up was no help. Bear knew that the mules were leaving tracks that any man could follow, but there was nothing he could do about that.

If Luther chose to pursue them, he would still have to hike back up higher to get to a place where he could cross the gorge. By evening, Bear and the girl would be well below, down into the valley and out of the trees.

"Once we're in the valley, Luther will be able to mount his horse and move faster in pursuit," Bear admitted out loud. "But if that is the path he chooses, we'll soon have ourselves a horse to ride."

Bear Le Vrette did not relish the thought of shooting Luther Corbett off the horse, but his guilt would be assuaged with a horse to ride across the valleys.

CHAPTER 16

Luther saddled all three horses and led them out of the corral. He had done what he could to make Seth Hanson comfortable, putting logs on the fire, leaving canteen and food within easy reach. He left the man a gun, too, to defend himself if bear or cougar wandered into the cabin. He had then rummaged through the cabin looking for things which might be useful to him, but found scant items. An old rope, a candle and lantern, a couple of potatoes and an onion that Old Bear must have left earlier in the day.

Luther was in sight of the cabin still when the thunder cracked and the rain started to fall. He pulled his hat down over his head a bit to help keep the rain out of his eyes, and he led the horses up along the path beside the cliff face overlooking the gorge, trying to hurry to the spot where he could cross the mountain stream and be on the right side of the gorge to follow Bear Le Vrette.

Luther's feelings toward the old mountain man had shifted hard during the course of the day. Finding the marshal's body and watching Seth Hanson get shot down was more than he could stand. Luther figured something vicious had tripped in Bear Le Vrette's mind. That's all that could explain Bear's actions over these past few days. The thought of his old friend losing his mind disturbed Luther. He lived in these mountains, same as Bear did, sheltered for days or weeks at a time through the winter, sometimes went months without seeing any soul other than Sally. Was it loneliness that made Old Bear crack? Was it too many winters?

Trappers and hunters had a tendency to start talking to themselves. They got irascible, short-tempered and grouchy, when they went below and encountered other people. The longer they were in the mountains, the worse they got.

And Luther was starting from a bad place. Old Bear and many of the other old timers had come to the mountains for the promise of money. Beaver pelt was like gold. Two or three good bearskins could buy a man all the supplies he would need to survive a whole year. Riches based on a life of outdoor toil in God's most glorious rock garden was what brought most all the others into the mountains. But Luther did not come for wealth from trapping and hunting. Luther came to the mountains because his mind was already broken. Four years of murder, that murder he committed and that murder he witnessed, had driven him away from his fellow man to a place of solitude and tranquility. Luther's mind was never right when he first came into the mountains.

And now he feared, as he hunted Bear Le Vrette, that he was equally hunting his own future. And the madness that drove Old Bear to steal this poor girl might come on sooner for Luther Corbett because he started so much closer to it.

These were hard contemplations, and Luther shook his head to clear his mind of them. He was not here to confront his past nor to face his future. He was here for the sole purpose of reclaiming this girl from a man who had no claim to her. And so Luther pressed on with a renewed determination. He'd made a promise to Seth Hanson, and he intended to do whatever it took to make good on that vow.

So he hurried the horses along, and once they were across the mountain stream, Luther mounted his horse and rode at a quicker pace down the big mountain slope toward the valley below. He tried not to think of the marshal dead at the bottom of the gorge or of Seth Hanson dying in Bear Le Vrette's old cabin. Instead, he imagined himself getting the girl and taking her home to her mother. He took comfort in these imaginings.

Luther came to these mountains to escape man's brutality toward man, and somehow the brutality had caught him here. Luther felt sick and enraged over the bloody violence that interrupted his solitude. He snapped the reins and rode harder.

Luther Corbett rode now with a new purpose. He'd been skeptical when the marshal and Seth Hanson first came to his cabin to enlist his help. He'd even thought his reason for being in the mountains was to intervene, to help his friend Bear Le Vrette. Corbett had thought there must have been a misunderstanding or perhaps Old Bear had suffered in his mind over the long winter.

Now, though, Luther rode having made a promise to a dying man to do right by the girl Lilly Grace Hanson. He did not ride for vengeance, he had no hatred for Bear Le Vrette, but he was bound to bring the girl, healthy and whole, back to her mother.

Finding the tracks in the rain soaked earth was no great challenge. Luther could easily see the trail left by the mules. Judging from the tracks and the time of the shooting, Luther figured Bear Le Vrette was not more than two hours ahead of him, and Luther's intended to press hard on Bear Le Vrette's trail in the hopes of catching him before sundown.

CHAPTER 17

As he descended into the valley, Bear Le Vrette kept near to the gorge cut by the mountain stream. Along the way, smaller creeks dumped into the gorge and the river began to cut a wider gap. Where he could, Le Vrette kept to the rocky ledge of the gorge where the roots of the spruce and mountain pines snaked across the face of the rocks in search for soil to penetrate and hold fast. And the reach of the roots proved successful, for the spruce and pine trees shot straight and high into the air like giant poles adorned at the top with green-needled branches.

They'd been moving lower for some time, at least a couple of hours, and Lilly Grace had not spoken. Le Vrette had her atop one of the mules because he believed they would move faster. The girl was still weak and still feeling poorly, but her health had improved as she grew accustomed to the hard traveling.

Bear's hope was that Luther Corbett would give up his chase. He did not understand how these other men had convinced Luther to assist them, but he was disappointed that his friend had joined the men chasing him.

But the old man's thoughts were not so much on why Luther Corbett chased him, but instead he was focused on how he would further his escape. Moving along the rocky ledge was helpful. Now that the rain had stopped, Bear knew that among the rocks the mules would not leave easy tracks to follow, but that mattered little. If Luther was going to persist in continuing the pursuit, he would be able to follow easy enough. There were tracks leading to the rocky ledge that followed the gorge, and Luther would then simply follow the river down into the valley.

Lilly Grace had not spoken since Old Bear fired the rifle. She never saw the results of the shot, but she was certain Old Bear had killed another man. As the sound of the exploding rifle grew fainter with each echo off the mountains, Lilly Grace believed her chances of salvation also grew fainter. Three men had now tried to stop Old Bear and been murdered for their efforts. Coggins at the store, stabbed to death while Old Bear held Lilly Grace's wrist in one hand; the injured man in the cabin, beaten and thrown over the edge of the gorge; and now someone else shot from across the gorge.

How many more men were there to even come to rescue her? Had there just been the two or were there more? And even if there were more, Lilly Grace wanted no one else to die on her behalf. The old man was cruel in the extreme, and terribly cunning. If more men came, Lilly Grace feared they would also fall at the hands of the old man.

They maneuvered down a steep slope that curved away from the gorge. The mules had difficulty making it as the trail dropped, but the old man led them slowly and carefully. At the bottom of the slope, they were level with the mountain stream, which had grown into a river, rushing violently in white foam over and between mountain rocks. The river roared loud here. They had gone all afternoon down the trail, and the light was beginning to grow dim.

"We ain't going to stop here," the old man said. "Ain't no way to watch our back trail from here. It'll start to get dark soon, but we'll push on a ways."

"Are there men still following us?" Lilly Grace asked, hopeful.

"One," Old Bear said. "One man still on our trail, unless he wised up and decided it warn't worth the pursuit."

Lilly Grace prayed that the single man still following them was her father. If not, her father was the victim of the gunshot.

They pressed on, following the course of the river. As they got deeper into the valley and the ground leveled out, the river beside them grew wider and gentler and flowed over pebbles instead of rushing over rocks. At times it meandered out into a small meadow and then back in among the thick cypress forests.

Though the water was almost like ice, Bear Le Vrette took spells when he led the mules out into the middle of the river and walked them through the water for long stretches, thinking to hide tracks. And at other times he would cross to one side or the other of the river and walk deep into the forest or out into a meadow, all the time trying to lead make tracks that would prove confounding for Luther. But he always returned to the shallows of the river to walk on the pebbles where he hoped to leave no trace.

But at last it came too dark to keep going, and Bear

Le Vrette stopped to make a camp in a meadow at the edge of the trees. He did not worry with shelter, instead making up a big fire to keep them warm. He made pine tea for the girl to help her keep up her strength, and he fried pemmican with onion and potato.

Bear Le Vrette's patience was wearing thin. He was tired of running and feeling irascible. Worse, Bear Le Vrette did not know where to go next. He could survive deeper in the mountains, but come winter he would need good shelter. For his age, Old Bear was strong, but not so strong that he could build a cabin alone in a few weeks and still trap and hunt sufficiently to provide stores for the winter. In his heart, he still wanted to return to the old cabin. But Luther Corbett had found the old cabin and had brought other men there. Bear Le Vrette could think of only way the old cabin would be made safe — a place where Old Bear could live out his remaining years with his wife in peace and without fear of interference from other men. If Bear and Caroline were to live in the old cabin again, Luther Corbett would have to be killed.

The girl slept fitfully. She was still weak and Bear grew concerned that she might have a fever. Rest was what she needed, but in the open and on the move, there was little chance for that.

A grunting noise and the shaking of leaves roused Old Bear as he dozed beside the girl with an arm over her so that so that she could not escape if he fell asleep. Bear sat up and listened. The grunts came again and then a third time. He knew for sure what it was he heard, and he cast another big log on the fire, and then another, to kick the flames up higher. He also checked his rifle to be sure it was loaded and primed.

Old Bear could not sleep. The mules were restless, too, and their periodic shifting about kept Bear awake. He added logs to the fire throughout the night. Deep and disturbing thoughts came to his mind, interrupted by rustling leaves somewhere not far off in the dark woods. Bear grew angrier that men would try to hunt him, that his own friend would not leave him in peace. He felt betrayed that Luther Corbett, a man he had befriended and taught like a son, would mount a pursuit of him. And try as he might, Bear Le Vrette could not imagine why these men pursued him. He had committed no crimes against these men. He just wanted to be left alone with Caroline, left to enjoy the remaining years alone with her in the mountains they loved. And the girl herself had turned sour on him. He did not understand why Caroline seemed to be in fear of him or what had happened to her tender touch or her musical laughter. He convinced himself that his wife must be suffering from a fever brought on by the vile men who hunted them.

Bear Le Vrette could not conceive that his mind had gone on him, that the thoughts he had were beyond reality. When his thoughts traipsed toward something rational, Old Bear would get confused again and remember how all seemed to be against him and his only hope was to get Caroline clear of these men and back to their old cabin.

And then, again, Bear's mind filled with dark thoughts of murder.

When the first gray light in the sky gave him something to see by, Bear left the girl asleep and roused himself.

The grunting he heard over night had led him to a plan.

Bear went through his packs until he found a seine he used whenever he was out trapping and wanted to easily catch fish for supper. He now strung it across the river, and in a short time he had in his net three smallmouth bass and a trout. They were all smallish fish, not much of a meal, but they would serve his purpose.

He packed up all of his supplies and tied the packs back onto the mules, but he tossed another log onto the fire to keep it burning good.

"Get up Caroline," Bear said, a rough urgency in his voice. "We ain't got much time."

The girl opened her eyes, though she'd already been awake. Lilly Grace felt too weak to move, but the old man bent over her and pulled her up to her feet. "Come on now," he said. "We ain't got much time before Luther will be here."

Bear made the girl walk, and he took the girl and the mules and led them up a steep incline to a ledge overlooking a bend in the river. He had seen the ledge as dawn broke. Now, up on the ledge, Bear looked as his line of sight down to the river. The location was perfect. He could get down behind a couple of large rocks and still be able to have a view down to the river. The girl and the mules could be pushed farther along the ledge where they would not be seen from the river. Everything here was ideal for his purposes.

"You stay here with the mules," Bear told the girl. "I'll be back in a jiffy."

Rifle in hand, Bear scaled down the slope and back to his campsite where he had left the fire burning and the fish sitting on a rock. Bear filleted the fish and laid them out on the rocks at the river bank. One of them he tossed onto the fire so that it's odor would permeate along the riverbank.

If Luther Corbett was as close behind as Bear believed, he would not have long to wait.

CHAPTER 18

Luther lit a candle inside the lantern he'd found in Bear Le Vrette's old cabin. The candle did not put off much light, but with it he was able to walk the horses and keep traveling even after dark. The forest was black, and branches often came from nowhere to jab him in the face as he walked through the dark forest. He could no longer follow tracks — the candle put off too dim a light for such an effort — but Luther was convinced that Bear would never stray too far from the river. Water is the most important thing to any man in the wilderness. Without water, a man in the mountains or the forests or the prairies or the desert will rapidly become dehydrated and be worthless. Though there were plenty of mountain streams, Luther was convinced that Bear would not leave this one. And so Luther kept an eye on the flowing water beside him and followed the river up on its bank. He led the horses, rather than try to ride, to avoid one of the horses stumbling into the river in the dark.

At times, Luther stopped to search the river bank for muddy hoof prints from the mules or other traces that would indicate he was still on the right track. Most of the time his searches were in vain, but a couple of times he discovered prints that told him he was still going in the right direction. The water was ankle deep in some places and knee deep in others, and it was so cold that Luther could not stand to be in it for long. But through the clear mountain water he found tracks in the riverbed itself that suggested Bear had walked through the water.

"He's a tough old man," Luther told the horses. "He'll not easily give up the girl."

At last, Luther could go no farther. He unsaddled the horses, cut a few spruce boughs for a bed, and rested under a blanket. But sleep did not come to him. Luther struggled to try to understand what devil had possessed his friend. The carnage of these last few days staggered him. Poor old Coggins, who charged unreasonable prices but was otherwise likable, stabbed to death while trying to defend an innocent girl from a man Coggins had known and trusted for years. The marshal, a strong and sturdy man who's body was shattered in its final hours. The evidence of the marshal's brutal death was something Luther Corbett never thought he would see again outside of his memories from the war. And Seth Hanson, gut shot in his desperate quest to save his daughter. Seth Hanson had been a wholly disagreeable man, arguing and casting suspicion at Luther as they tracked Old Bear. But the man was grieving and despairing over his abducted daughter, and his demeanor could be forgiven. Luther figured Hanson was now dead in Bear Le Vrette's old cabin, never to know if his daughter would be rescued. What evil took control of Bear's mind during this long winter, and was it a disease that every man of these mountains would one day encountered? Luther's night was tormented with these thoughts that would not leave his mind alone.

And so he was wrapped in his blanket with his eyes wide open when the first hints of gray light touched the sky beyond the dark spruce and mountain pines that reached so far toward the stars above.

Luther did not linger. He'd made no fire and so he cooked no breakfast. He saddled the horses and started back following the mountain stream, hoping that he would soon overtake Bear Le Vrette and the girl.

The landscape now was closer in. The river had cut its way deep into the valley floor and now flowed through a wide canyon in the valley with spruce and pine growing thick on each side of the river's banks and slopes rising beyond the trees on either side. Here along this stretch of the river there was no place for Bear to go to attempt to hide his tracks, for he would not easily make it up either slope with three mules. But there were ledges all along where Bear might climb and hide, and so Luther took his time as he walked along, leading the horses and watching these ledges and their slopes.

Alert for an opportunity for Bear to climb up out of this deep ravine, Luther was also aware that his old friend might also be lying in wait for him. Bear Le Vrette had already shot one man in ambush from distance, and so he might do it again.

The first gray light turned to blue dawn, but now the bright golden light of the rising sun was reaching down into the valley and beginning to add warmth to the day. Luther stopped for a bit and removed his wool coat and took some jerky from his bags to chew on as he went. The sweetness of the meat was more nourishing than the meal itself. And he thought his hunger was playing tricks on him when he first smelled the cooking fish, but as he continued on toward a bend in the river, he became sure that what he smelled was fish cooking over a fire.

One of the horses blowed agitation, and Luther turned to see it was his own paint horse that had grown concerned. Now all three horses were fidgety over something.

Someone was up ahead, around the bend in the river, cooking fish. It might be Bear Le Vrette and the girl. It almost surely had to be. But it could be a stranger, or another trapper the Luther might know. It was not a common thing, but Luther did sometimes encounter other trappers in the valleys below or on the upper slopes of the mountains. All the same, Luther decided to approach the river bend with the expectation that the man he sought was now found.

With the marshal's gun belt on his hip and his rifle in hand, Luther tied off the horses and moved forward at a crouch, picking his steps carefully so as not to stumble on a loose rock or break a fallen branch. He found it hard to believe that Old Bear would let hisself be so easily caught, but if exhaustion or guilt had forced Bear Le Vrette to surrender, Luther would be grateful for it.

As he came around the bend in the river, Luther could hear the crackling of the fire and smell the smoke before he saw it. Then up ahead, only a few yards in front of him, he now saw the fire burning.

The grizz, though, was behind a rock, and so sheltered that Luther did not see it until it lifted its enormous head and gave a curious snort.

Behind the big grizzly, Luther now saw the two cubs feasting on the fish filleted and left on a rock. Even with her cubs so near, Luther believed he might back away safely, for the massive she-bear gave no sign of charging. He slowly took a step backwards, and then another.

But this was the exact moment that Old Bear Le Vrette had been expecting. From his perch up on a ledge overlooking the bend in the river, he watched as Luther first spied the grizzly and halted in his tracks. Bear Le Vrette pulled the trigger on the rifle and sent a ball of lead into the grizzly's hind quarter, not a fatal shot, but one that was certain to excite the fury of the mama bear.

The crack of the rifle echoed all through that canyon, but the sound of it compared in no way to the terror of the grizzly's fury as she reared up, forelegs spread like massive, furred clubs, and her huge gaping mouth, with its horrendous teeth bared, let loose a horrifying roar. She drowned out the echo of the gun and gave voice to a new echo that shook the ground.

Luther Corbett did not have time to cock back the hammer on his rifle and raise it in his defense.

The mother bear charged, her massive shoulders swinging to and fro as she ran him down. Luther was paralyzed from fear, caught flat footed he did not move from the spot. And then she was upon him, a massive clawed foot swiping down at him with no more thought than Luther might give to swatting a fly.

Luther raised up the rifle in a weak effort to block the claw, but the grizz smacked the rifle from his hands and caught him a tremendous blow in the ribs that knocked him to the ground.

The grizz fell on top of him now, pinning him painfully to the ground with her vast weight. Luther threw his hands and arms behind his head to try to protect his head and neck. A bite from those massive teeth in the neck would be certain death. She might just as easily crush his skull with her jaws.

A tooth cracked into him above his ear, and it felt like mallet driving a wedge into his head. Immediately Luther's blood was flowing thick and sticky into his face.

Now she was biting down on his left forearm, and Luther thought sure his bones would snap like twigs.

His only hope was the marshal's revolver holstered on his thigh. With the bear trying to wrench his left forearm from his elbow, Luther reached down to his leg.

The pain was so intense that all Luther could see was a blinding white light that came from inside his own head, and he thought he would black out before he could save hisself.

His thumb felt for the hammer of the revolver and cocked it back. He felt it click on the half cock and then stop on the full cock. Behind his head, feeling and guessing, Luther twisted his wrist to try to get a shot off.

He pulled the trigger, but nothing happened. The percussion cap had come loose in the struggle, or maybe the marshal kept an empty chamber on his gun. Luther thumbed back the hammer again, and praying he had an aim on the bear, he pulled the trigger a second time.

This time the gun exploded, and Luther felt the weight of the grizz lift off him as she rolled away.

Luther scrambled to get up to a sitting position and he looked for the bear but could see nothing. His first thought was that she'd bit him so hard she'd popped his eyeballs, but his vision was like looking through mud, and Luther realized his eyes were thick with blood. His left arm was useless to him, so he wiped his eyes with the sleeve of his right arm, getting enough blood from his eyes that he could see a bit around him.

The mama bear was back up, perhaps only momentarily dazed by the sound of the gunshot so near to her ear, for she was rearing on her hind legs again, slobber and Luther's blood dripping from her mouth as she let loose another ferocious growl.

She was standing not four feet away, towering over him, preparing to fall down and renew her attack, and with her forelegs stretched wide, she presented a target that Luther could not miss, even with his eyes full of blood.

He thumbed back the hammer and fired a shot into her breast, and in quick succession he let her have another.

The great beast staggered backwards but did not fall.

Luther thumbed back the hammer again and this time placed his aim on the grizz's massive head. He fired a lead ball into her face, and the great bear stumbled and dropped to the ground.

Luther Corbett was battered.

He set the revolver on the ground beside him and sat still for several minutes, breathing hard and taking account of his injuries.

His eyes were too muddied over to see clear, so in his mind he tallied his hurts.

His legs were shaking like the devil, but otherwise uninjured. His left arm stung and was sore. She'd ripped the flesh pretty thorough and perhaps dislocated his shoulder, but he never heard the bones crack in her mouth.

The back of his head was sore and throbbing, and Luther could feel blood running down his neck. She'd torn a gash or two in his head.

In spite of himself, Luther could not help but chuckle a bit. He'd been in a life and death struggle with a grizz and faired better than a man might have cause to expect.

On shaky legs, Luther pushed himself up off the ground and stood for a moment. The fear had not left him, and he was quivering from bloody head to toe.

Luther untucked his shirt and used the front tail of it to pull his left forearm up against his body. He held the shirt and arm against himself and stumbled over to the creek. There, he let his left arm dangle in the icy water and cupped water with his right hand to wash his eyes and face. Then he washed the back of his head in the same manner, but he just saw more and more blood pour into the river.

Without thought of rifle or revolver, Luther stumbled back to the horses, and there he took a rolled blanket from one of the saddles and cut it into strips. He had only his right hand and teeth and feet to work with, and it made it hard to do anything, but he managed to tie a strip of blanket tight around his head in the hopes of stopping the bleeding.

His shoulder felt like fire, and Luther knew he had to figure some way to get his shoulder back into place. But the predicament was made doubly serious by the terrible gashes to his forearm. The bear had mauled his left arm. All the same, he tied a rope to his left wrist, tossed the other end of the rope over a tree branch, and then pulled the rope with his right hand, raising his left arm in the process, until he heard it clunk back into place.

He wet a strip of the blanket in the cold stream and wrapped it loosely around his left arm where the grizz had chewed it like a piece of jerky. Then he took another strip of the blanket and tied a sling around his neck to hold his arm up.

Treating his own injuries was tedious and time consuming. He was weak with blood loss, and his entire body trembled.

When he was at last finished, Luther took out some tobacco and bit off a chunk that he pushed into his cheek. Then he hollered out at the mountains, "You did not get me Bear Le Vrette! I am still coming for you!"

CHAPTER 19

Luther walked the horses out past the bear. The cubs had gone, disappeared back into the woods, and even though the mother grizzly was sprawled dead on the ground, Luther walked with trepidation as he passed her. The horses, too, were none too pleased about being led past the dead bear. Luther was disturbed to see the marks from the fight. His own blood stained the dirt where he had fought the bear.

He fetched his rifle and the revolver, and he took the time to reload the revolver and put percussion caps on the nipples of each chamber. The chore was all the more difficult with his injured left arm immobile against his chest, but Luther felt it was a necessary job. Purposefully wounding a grizzly bear so that it would attack was a vicious and cruel gambit, and Luther feared the mind that could conceive of such a ploy.

From the river bank, Luther examined the ledge from which Old Bear had been perched. He saw that the ledge ran for quite a distance, but it appeared that it eventually sloped up higher into the valley and out of the gorge by the river. There were plenty of tracks indicating that Bear had taken the mules up the slope to the ledge, and none to suggest he'd brought them back down again. So Luther led the horses up the steep incline to the ledge.

At the top of the ledge, Luther turned to take a last look at the bear and admire Bear Le Vrette's vantage point. Luther saw now how Bear had set the trap, leaving fish on a rock to lure the mama bear and her cubs, watching from behind these rocks, then with a clear line of sight shooting the bear to wound but not kill. It seemed a pitiful waste to just leave the mama grizz there and take neither meat nor hide. Even with the bullet holes, she could still make a good skin. Two cubs had been orphaned and a fine grizz destroyed to no purpose. Luther would almost have preferred that Old Bear had just shot him.

But too much time had already passed.

Luther was weak from the fight with the grizzly and the loss of blood. He needed to get the horses up to level ground where he could ride rather than walk and close the distance on Bear Le Vrette. The sooner he caught up to Old Bear, the less likely there would be further surprises waiting him.

Old Bear had made no further effort to hide his tracks, plainly assuming that there would be no further pursuit. The trail was easy enough to follow, and indeed the ledge did rise to meet the valley, but as Luther climbed up out of the canyon and reached the valley, he was perplexed to see that the tracks turned back the way he'd come, now moving upstream of the river below.

Luther suspected that here was another ruse, Old Bear trying to throw him off the trail. But he had no choice other than to follow the tracks. Now, though, he could mount up on his paint horse and ride, saving his strength and resting a bit before what he knew would be his final fight with Bear Le Vrette.

The valley was scattered with wide meadows and open forests, and Luther found that he was able to move along at a good pace. There were signs enough to allow him to know that he was still riding in the right direction, and Luther came to believe that Bear was determined still to return to the old cabin. He had turned back in the valley and intended to meet the river again upstream and follow it back up the mountain.

When he first set out with the marshal and Seth Hanson, Luther intended to intervene on Old Bear's behalf. He was sure, then, that some terrible misunderstanding had occurred, and he would prevent the marshal and Hanson from exacting justice in kind. But Luther Corbett's mind had swung the other way now. There could now be no doubt that Old Bear had done murder — Luther had seen it himself — and Luther believed whatever came next would surely be a killing.

Luther had been riding for perhaps three-quarters of an hour when, at last, the trees opened up into a big meadow of luscious green grass and white and yellow wildflowers, and half a mile in front of him Luther saw the three mules, the old man and the girl.

He halted his horse and sat for a moment, taking in the surroundings. Bear Le Vrette did not yet know it, but he had come to the end of his trail. For one of these two men, this meadow would be their last view. Luther was determined that he would survive the encounter and that Bear Le Vrette would not.

Luther considered that he might make a dash through the open meadow, run down on Bear, but that seemed a foolhardy way to go about it. Had not Luther seen the carnage from a charge across wide open fields?

What he needed now was to get in front of Bear Le Vrette and let Bear stumble onto him. Seth Hanson had fallen victim to an ambush. Luther had been torn up when Old Bear used a grizzly to ambush him. It was now time to work Bear's tactics against him.

The forest curled its way around the meadow, and so Luther decided he would ride just inside the tree line. The big arc of trees around the meadow was long, but Bear and the mules were moving at a slow pace. Luther believed he could ride the tree line and get to the opposite side of the meadow before Old Bear could finish his journey across. He tied off the other two horses inside the tree line so they did not wander out into the meadow and alert Bear, and then Luther charged ahead on his horse, riding fast among the trees.

It was painful business. Each hoof fall rattled his throbbing head and jarred his aching shoulder, but Luther gritted his teeth and pressed on. Whenever there was a gap in the trees, Luther spared a glance into the meadow to be certain that Old Bear was not out-pacing him, but each time he saw the old man was still moving slow. Luther decided this was evidence that Old Bear was suffering exhaustion, too. He'd been hunted for days now, and it was no easy going up through the mountains and down into this valley. The old man was tired and weak, and that would only serve to help Luther in what was to come next.

As Luther rounded the arc of trees to the side of the meadow where Old Bear would soon enter back in among the trees, he rode a bit deeper into the forest so that he could get up ahead of Bear Le Vrette.

Satisfied that he had at last ridden deep enough into the woods and come to a point that would intersect with Old Bear's path, Luther dismounted and drew his rifle from its scabbard.

He left the paint horse loose, he knew it would not wander far, and now Luther stealthily began to pick his way back toward the meadow to meet Old Bear. Luther came to a small clearing surrounded by tall mountain pines and decided this would be the place. He crouched behind a thick fir tree and waited.

But the minutes ticked by, and Old Bear did not appear in the clearing. Luther was certain that Bear would come this way, but even moving as slow as he was, Old Bear should have arrived already at the clearing. Luther peered through the tall tree trunks for any sign of movement, but only squirrels seemed to be out. After several minutes of anxious waiting, Luther decided to creep farther forward. Picking his way from tree to tree and keeping his eyes open and his ears listening, Luther continued to move forward without picking up any sign from Bear.

Had the old man turned around? Did he see the horses among the trees on the opposite side of the meadow? Luther's heart pounded in his chest as he tried to figure what had delayed his old friend.

Finally, nearing the edge of the forest, Luther saw that Old Bear had stopped in the meadow. He and the girl were eating and the mules were grazing.

Luther saw, too, that Old Bear's rifle was leaned against the branch of a small scrub oak out in the meadow. So he stepped forward, out of the cover of the trees, and into the meadow where he knew, for one of the two men, this would be their last ever view of the mountains they both loved.

CHAPTER 20

"That trick with the bear was a poor way to treat a man," Luther said, his tone genial.

Lilly Grace and Bear Le Vrette both started at the words that broke the silence. Lilly Grace was horrified by the bloodied, bandaged man standing before them with his arm in a sling. Luther Corbett's beard was matted with blood. Big swaths of his white shirt were stained a muddy-red where he had bled all over himself. If this was the deliverance for which she had prayed, she was forced to concede that the instruments of God sometimes came in unholy attendance.

Old Bear laughed as if the whole thing had been just a joke. "We've been friends so long, it didn't hardly seem right to just shoot you."

Luther took a step forward and winced at the pain in his arm. He was holding the rifle with one hand and it was vaguely pointing toward Bear Le Vrette, but he realized now that it would be damned difficult to aim, cock and fire it with one hand. He considered tossing it to the ground and drawing the pistol from the holster, but he did not want to give Bear any chance.

"Tell me why you've done these things, Bear," Luther said. "I need to understand."

Old Bear wrinkled his face in concentration as if he did not fully comprehend the question. After a moment, though, he said, "I just wanted to be left alone with Caroline. I'm an old man, and I have earned my peace."

"But this girl is not Caroline," Luther said.

"Don't say such," Bear shot back, and his tone quickly turned dark.

"Caroline has been dead so many years now, Bear. You have to know this is not Caroline."

"Don't say such," Bear growled. "Don't say such, Luther Corbett. You never knew Caroline."

Luther looked at the girl. She was sitting in the tall grass, a bit of uneaten jerky in her hand. She appeared pale and weak.

"What's your name, girl?" Luther asked her.

In a small voice she answered, "Lilly Grace Hanson."

"There. You see, Bear. Lilly Grace is her name. Not Caroline. She's not Caroline at all."

"Don't say such, Luther Corbett. It ain't often a man gets a second chance. I'll not have you take that away from me."

"It's no second chance, Bear," Luther said, and he his heart was full of sorrow for his friend. "You're confused. But in your confusion, you've done terrible things. There has to be a reckoning for that."

Bear Le Vrette concentrated hard as he tried to remember what terrible things he had done. He only knew that he had been reunited with the woman he loved and that men had chased them and that Caroline was sickly on account of these men. These men led by his very own friend.

"There will be a reckoning," Bear agreed, his voice a snarl. His face contorted to rage, and Bear Le Vrette charged forward toward Luther Corbett.

Luther was thrown off guard. Bear was coming at him just as that mama grizz had done, and in a moment of panic, Luther fired off the rifle. The shot missed, and Bear Le Vrette was nearly atop him.

With his one good arm, Luther swung the rifle like a club and caught Old Bear in the side of the head. Bear reeled for a moment and Luther backed away, tossing the rifle to the ground.

Luther bared his teeth in a snarl and rushed toward the old man, but Bear Le Vrette's age belied his strength. As they came together like two great rams, Bear took Luther by the shoulders and flung him bodily to the ground. Luther landed heavy on the earth and struggled to catch his breath. His shoulder was on fire again from where Bear had grabbed it, and Luther had a sudden surge of fear as he realized he was too weak and too busted up to fight the old man.

Bear drew the long bladed knife from his belt and came at Luther again, but Luther was on the ground on his back, and when Bear got close enough Luther kicked out and bashed the old man in the gut. Bear Le Vrette was staggered for a moment and stood breathing hard.

Luther scrambled to his feet. The marshal's revolver

on his thigh was an unnatural appendage, and he did not immediately think of it.

Instead, Luther thought of his long friendship with Old Bear. He had walked into this meadow with the intention of killing Old Bear, but now he was not sure he could do it. Even faced with the knowledge that Bear Le Vrette would likely kill him if he had the opportunity, Luther now balked at the thought of murdering his friend.

"I do not wish to fight you, Bear Le Vrette," Luther said. "But I cannot allow you to continue to hold this girl. Turn her loose and let her come with me, and you can go on in peace."

"I'll not do it," Old Bear growled. "We're going back to our cabin, together."

Lilly Grace Hanson picked up the rifle from where it was leaning against the tree, and she cocked back the hammer. She leveled the long gun at Bear Le Vrette. Her father had taught her to shoot, and she hunted deer and rabbit. This gun was bigger than anything she had shot before, but she was sure she could use it.

"I'm not going to that cabin with you," Lilly Grace said behind the long barrel of the musket.

Bear turned away from Luther Corbett and looked at the girl with his gun pointed at him.

"Caroline?" he said, and there was a questioning hurt to his tone. "Caroline?" he repeated.

Luther watched the tragedy play out in front of him. He saw the confusion and the hurt writ in the wrinkles of Bear Le Vrette's face. He heard the heartache in his voice.

Whatever illness had taken hold of Bear Le Vrette's

mind, it was complete. He'd let it get into his brain that this girl was his dead wife — resurrected to live out a fantasy of the old man's imagination. And to make good that fantasy, Old Bear Le Vrette had killed three good men.

Luther's courage failed him at the critical moment. Even facing his own death, he did not have the courage to shoot down his old friend — a man who no longer was his old friend. A man whose mind had endured too many lonely winters in the mountains. Yet where Luther's courage failed, this young, frail girl stood fast. She was willing to do the thing that Luther had been unwilling to do.

But Luther had shot men, and he knew what killing was and what it did not just to the victim but to the killer. He understood that if Lilly Grace Hanson pulled that trigger she would be forever changed, if she wasn't already. So in the final moment, when the reckoning had to come and there was no other choice, Luther drew the marshal's six-shooter and fired. It was an act of mercy to the girl he'd sought to save. It was an act of mercy to the friend he'd sought to save. Hearing the hurt in Old Bear's voice and understanding how thoroughly broken the man's mind had become, Luther saw no other way than to bring an end to the suffering. With the marshal's gun, Luther Corbett settled Bear Le Vrette's accounts. All of them.

CHAPTER 21

Lilly Grace Hanson never again saw the man who saved her. She never did know his name. She did not know why he risked his life for her or why he killed the man he called a friend. She did not know of the promise that Luther Corbett made to her father when Seth Hanson was on his deathbed.

For four days they tracked back through the mountains, riding horses and trailing mules. Lilly Grace could not say if they moved along the same trail that had taken them so deep into the wilderness or the man who rescued her forged out a new path. All the rocks looked the same as the other rocks, the trees looked the same as the other trees, and the bald mountains all looked one just like the next.

The man was hurt bad. His bandaged arm remained slung against his chest and the couple of times he had Lilly Grace change out his bandages, and the arm looked like raw beef run through a meat grinder. His head was also badly gashed, and it would sometimes start bleeding again, seemingly without cause.

Still, with his one good arm, the man led the horses and mules along perilously narrow ledges, chopped spruce boughs for lean-to shelters, made fires and even hunted rabbits and squirrel so that they had fresh meat for suppers.

"This horse I'm riding is my daddy's horse," Lilly Grace said at the campfire on the first night.

"It is," the man agreed.

"Is my daddy killed?" she asked.

"He is," the man told her. "Shot by that man Bear Le Vrette."

Lilly Grace felt a deep pit of hurt in her heart, but she had no tears to give. She would cry for her father later, but not now.

The man who saved her took care of Lilly Grace on their return journey. He saw to it that she was warm and fed, and as a result, she quickly began to have some energy again. He made for her the same piny tea that the other man had made, but now it seemed to work better to give her strength.

He did not talk overly much, but he told her throughout the trip where they were going next so that she could mark their progress in her mind. "Up over this ridge and around that mountain yonder," he would say. "Then we'll drop down into a valley and have just one more mountain to cross."

As they rode through a meadow, she saw him wince and start when his horse stepped heavily in a low depression.

"Are you terribly hurt?" she asked.

"I'll survive it," he said.

"What happened to your arm?"

"I was attacked by a grizz."

"Is that why he laid out those fish? The morning before you saved me, the old man caught some fish and laid them out. Then we waited a long time watching our campsite. Then he fired a shot and we left."

"That's right," the man said. "Old Bear laid a trap for me. That shot was him shooting the grizzly enough to make her angry but not enough to kill her. He did that just as I came into view, and she charged me."

"Is that what happened to your head, too?"

"It is. That grizz did a number on me."

"Was that man — Old Bear — was he a friend of yourn?"

"He was."

"Why did he take me?"

"I reckon I don't know," the man said. "Winters in these mountains can be hard on a man. He seemed to have it in his mind that you were his wife, but she died a long time ago, before I ever even knew him. Maybe you favor her in some way. Maybe he saw you and just got it in his head wrong that you was her."

"I'm sorry you had to kill your friend," Lilly Grace said.

The man rode quietly for a minute or two, pondering the killing. "I reckon he needed it."

After four days of riding and walking through the

135

mountains, they came down into the valley where Coggins store was. "I suppose you'll have to lead the way from here," the man said. "Do you know where your home is?"

"I can lead the way," Lilly Grace said.

Lilly Grace's brothers were working in the fields in front of the home when she rode up. One of them came to her and helped her down from the horse and watched the man who saved her with suspicion as he dismounted. The other brother ran to the house and fetched her mother.

Her mother wrapped Lilly Grace in her arms, the woman's face red and tears streaming down her cheeks. "I prayed that you would be delivered back to us," the mother sobbed into Lilly Grace's hair.

The boys, Lilly Grace's two brothers, stood by on shifting feet. The unasked question plain on their faces. They wanted to know where their pa was.

Inside the farm cabin, Lilly Grace's mother made her lie down in bed. She stroked the girl's hair and face, tucked her into her blankets and stalled any other way she could think to stall. But eventually she had to go out and face the stranger who'd brought her daughter home. Like her sons, she already expected the terrible news he would deliver. At length, though, she could make him wait no longer. Mrs. Hanson went outside where she talked for a long time with the man who'd saved Lilly Grace; both her sons stood by with sullen faces and listened. Lilly Grace climbed from bed and went to a window where she tried to listen to the conversation. She could only hear parts of it. The man talked in low tones. He told the woman that her husband was killed and a marshal, too. He described some of the events without offering details. He told her Bear Le Vrette was killed.

Lilly Grace heard the man say that he intended to go back and bury Seth Hanson.

Luther stepped back up into his saddle, intending to get going again, but the girl came running from the cabin.

"Are you going to bury my daddy?" She did not cry. Her voice did not break. It was a simple, straight question from a child who had endured too much already.

"I am," Luther said.

"Will you say a prayer over his grave?"

"I reckon I can do that."

***

Luther Corbett left the marshal's horse and Hanson's horse and Bear Le Vrette's mules with Hanson's wife. Her life was about to get much harder. Though her sons were old enough to work the farm, these mountains and their valleys were no place for a woman with children and no husband, and Luther had regret that Hanson had been killed and there was naught he could do about it.

Luther was nearer home now than he'd been for the better part of two weeks. He was exhausted and shattered, but Luther Corbett felt his responsibility to the dead was not yet lifted and so he delayed his return home. He had buried Bear Le Vrette in a shallow grave and piled up rocks to keep the animals from digging him up. But Seth Hanson was lying dead in Bear's old cabin, and Luther had to see to that man's body before he could see to hisself. Alone in the mountains and sure of his destination, Luther traveled faster than he had done before, and was back to Bear Le Vrette's old cabin in two days.

The corpse on the cot was untouched by scavenging

animals, and Luther was relieved to find it as such.

Digging a grave with one arm in half-frozen, half-rock ground was a tiresome chore. His ribs ached, his shoulder was painful, and his head throbbed with every exertion. Luther found a pick-ax that he used to loosen the dirt, and he shoveled out a shallow bed as best he could. The grave was more shallow than he'd have liked, but when it was deep enough to suffice, Luther wrapped Seth Hanson's corpse in a blanket and dragged it out to the grave. He shoveled the dirt back over the body and then covered the grave with rocks.

Luther did not go much for sentimentality. He did not speak to the dead man, did not tell Seth Hanson that he had fulfilled his promise to return the stolen daughter. But when he'd placed the last of the rocks over the grave, he took off his hat, held it over his chest and bowed his head.

"Lord, I ain't much for praying. I done all I could for this man. Now, I reckon, it's up to you to do what you can for his soul."

He knew that he would not be able to do anything for the marshal's body. There was no way for him to get down into the gorge. And when he looked for it, it was gone anyway. Dragged off by the water in the river or maybe by wolves that found a way down to it. Luther decided it was a sad and unfitting end for a man who seemed decent enough.

The trail of the violence that had come to these mountains was pretty well covered over now. Though here and there evidence remained, the best of trackers would not be able to follow the trail and deduce what befell the men in the graves. If he thought on it for a thousand years, Luther would never be able to explain what compelled Old

Bear Le Vrette to steal Lilly Grace Hanson from her family and set in motion this chain of events that ended with so much murder and sadness. Luther was forced to accept it was some sickness of the mind in Old Bear and that it was brought on by solitude and loneliness in a long winter. Too much loneliness, and too long the winter.

The sun dropped below the far mountain and shortly the sky turned fiery orange, gray, and then black. Luther watched it all from a log bench outside of Bear's old cabin. He liked this place, with the water running in the gorge below and mountains across the way. It was a rugged beauty, and maybe it was not meant for man. Maybe Old Bear and Caroline and Luther and Sally, the Hansons and the marshal and the store keeper Coggins — maybe they'd all come to a place God did not intend for them to be, and they had reaped their punishments for trespassing.

Luther leaned his head back against the wall of the cabin and slept there for a long while before the cold woke him. Then he went inside the cabin and slept on the floor under his blanket. He did not want to sleep on the cot where Seth Hanson had died.

In the morning he saddled his paint horse and rode back toward home. It took two days, but he now knew the way and felt he could ride it in the dark. His longing for home was severe, Luther felt it in his chest like a gnawing hunger, and when he entered into the valley meadow he let the paint gallop even though it caused hurt to his shoulder and ribs and intensified the ache in his head. At last he saw the grove of Quaking Aspen among the spruce and then he was crossing the creek and entering the clearing below the arced stone wall.

Sally was out in the field, pulling weeds from the

garden. The windows of the cabin were open, and the skins that carpeted the floor were hanging on a line strung between two skinny aspen trunks. The clearing was green and lush, and Sally was like a vision with her black hair and tan skin.

She came to him as he nearly fell from the saddle. She did not speak, for Sally never was one for much talking, but she looked him over, gently laying fingers on his bandaged head and slung arm. Her eyes showed both concern and relief.

Luther Corbett's traps were still hanging from the wall of his cabin, empty of game. He would have to get them out soon if he was going to get skins this summer.

But not now. Now, Luther allowed Sally to lead him into the cabin. He let her unwrap the bandages. She winced when she looked at his arm, but she made up a salve of honey that she spread on the wounded arm and into the ragged cut on the back of his head.

Sally led him to the bed where he laid down on his back while she wrapped a new, clean bandage around his arm. Luther's eyes grew heavy under Sally's gentle touch as she brushed the hair away from his face and softly brushed her lips against his forehead. The traps and skins could wait, Luther concluded, as Sally's tender care swept him off to sleep.

THE END

THANK YOU!

Thank you so much for reading
TOO LONG THE WINTER!

If you enjoyed the book, please consider leaving a review. I really appreciate feedback from readers, and it helps me to know how to focus future writing efforts when readers let me know what I got right (or even where I missed the mark) with my stories.

If you enjoyed "Too Long the Winter," I would encourage you to check out some of the other Western and Frontier Adventure novels I have written, and periodically check my website (robertpeecher.com) for updates.

Luther Corbett's adventures in the Colorado Territory have not finished. While "Too Long the Winter" is not part of an ongoing series, Luther Corbett will appear again in future writings in the Animas Forks series scheduled for release in the Spring of 2018.

If you have not yet, please sign up for my newsletter at robertpeecher.com and follow my Facebook page "Robert Peecher Novels," and you can be among the first to know when I have new releases.

ABOUT THE AUTHOR

When he's not living in the 1800s through his Western and Civil War fiction, Robert Peecher is often found paddling rivers, hiking trails, sending lead down range, spending time with his three sons, or hanging out with his first reader, best friend, and wife Jean.

OTHER NOVELS BY ROBERT PEECHER

THE LODERO WESTERNS: Lodero is a gunslinger bent on keeping a graveside promise to his mother: To find out what happened to his father who set off to seek a fortune and all that ever came home was an empty trunk.

ANIMAS FORKS: Animas Forks, Colorado, is the largest city in America (at 14,000 feet). The town has everything you could want in a Frontier Boomtown: cutthroats, ne'er-do-wells, whores, backshooters, drunks, thieves, and murderers. And there's also some unsavory folks who show up.

JACKSON SPEED: Scoundrels are not born, they are made. The Jackson Speed series follows the life of a true coward making his way through 1800s America – from the Mexican American War through the Civil War and into the Old West. "The history is true and the fiction is fun!"

FIND THESE AND OTHER NOVELS BY
ROBERT PEECHER AT AMAZON.COM

Made in United States
North Haven, CT
21 September 2022

24404135R00093